SHORT STUFF

A Young Adult LGBTQ+ Anthology

Edited by Alysia Constantine

interlude press • new york

ISBN 13: 978-1-945053-89-4 (trade)
ISBN 13: 978-1-945053-90-0 (ebook)
LCCN: 2020934448

Published by Interlude Press
www.interludepress.com

Book and Cover Design by CB Messer
Photography for Cover © Depositphotos.com/mjth
10 9 8 7 6 5 4 3 2 1

interlude ✦✦ press • new york

CONTENTS

Introduction: On Ending Up Happy 1
I Ate the Whole World to Find You 5
The August Sands.. 53
Love in the Time of Coffee.. 106
Gilded Scales 145

INTRODUCTION: ON ENDING UP HAPPY

I LOVE A GOOD MEET-CUTE story. You know the kind: On first meeting, two would-be lovers dislike each other, but they eventually fall in love. Someone is usually a jerk in the beginning. Someone misunderstands something. Circumstances conspire to make things worse. The should-be lovers, against their wishes, are thrown together and must muddle through somehow. During all that muddling, the improbable couple falls in love. It's a convention full of hope—tough beginnings make happy endings.

Maybe that's why the meet-cute is so right for stories of LGBTQ folks: We usually find ourselves in tough beginnings. Then circumstances conspire to make things really hard on us. Falling in love happens against all odds.

But darn it if we don't deserve our happy endings too.

My wife and I had our own meet-cute story. I was a young professor, and she was a new therapist at the university's counseling center. She wanted to start an LGBTQ student group, and several folks told her to contact me to do it, since I'd already started a women's center on campus and was a generally gung-ho kind of professor. But our first meeting went off the tracks—she showed up on the wrong day, and I wasn't even on campus. Then, thinking she'd showed up on the right day but had been stood up by me, she stood me up on the day I *was* there. As a result, when we finally met, we were both cranky and a little rude to each other.

Luckily for both of us, we realized the mishap, and she invited me over to watch a movie and help fix up a couple of her friends. During all the matchmaking machinations, my future-wife and I clicked, and we've been together ever since—eighteen years and counting. (I'm not sure if Kyle and Stephen are still together, but I hope they are.)

I'm sure my wife would tell this story differently—I'm sure in her version, the mistakes were mine, not hers, and I was probably somehow a jerk. But I have the pen right now, so I get to be the decider of everything. That's the power of telling a story: How it happens and what it means is up to you.

It's not far off from how it feels to write your *own* love story, if you choose to do it. LGBTQ people cannot always rely on the old love story scripts because our plotlines are often very different from the most common traditional ones, with unique pleasures and dangers. Most of the old love stories don't apply to us, unless we bend them to fit. For instance, when legal marriage was not a possibility, we made our own traditions of faithfulness. When our families and communities rejected us, we made our own families out of those who did accept and care for us. LGBTQ folks have always had to keep a grain of salt in our pockets.

Until recently, we haven't had the opportunity to tell—or read—stories about ourselves at all. Having few models in literature, movies, or even in our own lives to show how it can be is tough, but it also gives us great opportunity to write our *own* stories. We're not limited by readymade models. We had to get creative. Nobody has to be a helpless princess or a tirelessly ⌐hing prince. Nobody *really* needs those models, but because ⌐els often don't fit us at all, it's easier to see we don't need them. We don't even need a "happily ever after," as long as we're happy.

Each of the stories in this collection, in its own way, is a "meet-cute" story. First, there's the classic versions, in which two people meet under impossible circumstances but wind up falling in love. In "I Ate the Whole World to Find You" by Tom Wilinsky and Jen Sternick, a budding chef meets a crotchety Olympic swimming hopeful and wins him over by cooking delicious, specially crafted meals. In Jude Sierra's "August Sands," two boys on the verge of adulthood (college, independent lives) meet and fall in love while on one last vacation with their families. Falling in love, however, is only the beginning—they have to decide whether to cling to each other or dive alone into the unwritten future. In both of these classic "meet-cute" stories, big life changes loom on the horizon. Deciding to let yourself fall in love in the shadow of those big changes is daunting, a bit dangerous, brave.

"Love in the Time of Coffee" by Kate Fierro takes the basic idea of Gabriel Garcia Marquez's *Love in the Time of Cholera* (friends separated by another love interest, then reunited in newfound passion) and turns it on its toes. Now two best friends, Gemma and Anya, learn to see past boy-craziness and convention to meet each other anew as lovers.

Finally, Julia Ember's "Gilded Scales" roams furthest from the classic "meet-cute" story—it's more of a classic "girl-meets-dragon" tale. You know the old formula: a would-be warrior is barred from combat because she is a girl; through a series of mishaps, she meets a dragon and romance ensues. Okay, it's not exactly an old formula, and you probably don't know it, but I don't want to give away too much of the story. It *is* the tale of a very unlikely couple, and of how real love can rescue you from the palest prison of a life, even if it doesn't look like everybody else's idea of love.

The thing that holds all "meet-cute" stories together is hope. Love, in all its forms, is always an act of hope. It means you're willing to leap unprotected into the future, to risk safety and familiarity to be with another person. This can be especially true for LGBTQ people, who often have much farther to leap.

Things may look dire, but we are powerful people. Things may be darkest before dawn, but we don't need to wait for the sun to rise; we can turn on a light. We can rewrite the old stories. Tough beginnings make happy endings. We can make our own happiness and we don't have to slay a dragon to do it.

—Alysia Constantine, January 2020

ABOUT THE EDITOR: Alysia Constantine is a critically acclaimed author whose novels blur the line between reality and fantasy, feature luscious prose and explore complex themes of otherness. Her novels *Sweet* (Interlude Press, 2016) and *Olympia Knife* (Interlude Press, 2017) received starred reviews from *Publishers Weekly* and *Foreword Reviews*, respectively. She lives in the Lower Hudson Valley with her wife, two dogs, and a cat and is a former professor at a New York arts college.

I ATE THE WHOLE WORLD TO FIND YOU

by Tom Wilinsky and Jen Sternick

4:30 A.M. WE ARE OUT of Strawberry Milkshake Pop-Tarts.

Dad is already in the car, listening to NPR. I sling my gym bag, emblazoned with the black Submergd fin and weighed down by two water bottles, sunscreen, goggles, my workout notebook, and two swim caps, over my shoulder. The only thing in there without a Submergd logo on it is the pair of neon-orange lifeguard trunks. Usually, on the way out the door, I add two Pop-Tarts to the top to eat during the ride, but the box in my hand is empty.

4:32 a.m. I grab a couple of granola bars and a jar of peanut butter. This is a bad start to the day.

During the drive, Dad mutters at the radio while I dip the granola bars in the peanut butter and eat them. I review the workout notes Koji gave me last night. *Starts. Fly to back transition. Sprints.* At the bottom of the page is the note *Contact Mr. Taplin to set up WUA interview,* with a number. This is the fifth day that item has been in my notes.

As if he's reading over my shoulder, Dad asks, "Did you call yet?"

When my parents signed the official sponsor paperwork with Submergd last winter, the company made it very clear that I can only train and compete in Submergd gear, I am not allowed to wear clothing with a Submergd competitor's logo (Leo Taplin helpfully provided a written list of forbidden brands), and I must participate in scheduled media appearances, including a half-hour, in-depth biopic on *Wake-Up America!* in their New York City studios to kick off "Meet America's Next Olympians" week.

I groan, wedging the last bit of peanut butter-laden granola bar out of the jar. It's delicious. I'm going to pay for this.

"I haven't made the Olympic team yet. Trials aren't for weeks. I don't see why I have to do this now."

"Basil, we've been over this. The interviews are part of the package. They need to start building interest in you to get the most from their investment. I know you hate hearing the M word, but—"

"Okay, okay, I got it. I'll call him, all right?" Three years ago, after I broke the Under-15s Individual Medley national record, we moved halfway across Connecticut so that I could live closer to Koji. We need the Submergd endorsement money for his coaching fees. I'm being a brat. I mumble an apology as Dad pulls through the gates of the Upper Collingford Swim Club and drops me in front of the pool.

4:42 a.m. My gut churns. The peanut butter was a mistake. I can't keep making those. I don't have time to think about facing a camera lens, fumbling to explain how I know when to start my flip turn, and, worse, having to listen to the constant comparisons. "You have a six-foot, seven-inch wingspan, just like Michael Phelps. You're double-jointed, just like—" I rush through the club, drop the Submergd track shorts, and scramble for goggles. I'm in the pool at 4:46.

"Late," is Koji's only comment.

*   *   *

Two and a half hours later, my solo practice ends, and my teammates wander in to warm up. As Koji drones through the day's practice focus, I stare at the metal corrugated cover of the pool snack bar—still closed. All I can think about is eggs. And bacon. Pancakes with maple syrup. Orange juice. I eat two protein bars, a banana, and a bag of trail mix I swipe from one of the girls.

Team practice starts at 7:30. Back in the water.

I argue with Koji about back work. He punishes me for being late this morning by not letting me work on anything else.

"A minute," I say, "I was one minute late. Let me do one free for every two back. You know I hate back."

"'You hate it because you're bad at it," he snaps. "Get better and you won't hate it."

As soon as Koji releases the team at 8:45, I head to the snack bar while tugging a Submergd tank top over my head. *Thank God, it's finally open.* Part of my deal with the club is that I get all the food I want, every shift.

The cook behind the grill is new and about my age. He's chopping an onion so fast I'm scared for his fingers. He's got what my mother would call a Roman nose and bluish-gray eyes. He's really focused on that onion until I put my hand on the counter. He looks vaguely familiar, as if we've met before, but I don't know him. He knows me, though.

"Hey, good workout?" he says, as if we're friends. This happens more and more. People who never speak to me at school come up and fist bump me at the lifeguard chair. Girls ask for selfies. My parents' neighbors bring their kids to say hi and explain that I'm training at Upper Collingford for the Olympics.

He wears a real chef's jacket, not just an apron, and black-and-white checkered pants. He's shorter than I am—I'm guessing he's not quite six feet tall—and a little heavyset. His dark hair is almost buzz-cut, and he cracks eggs one-handed into a huge metal bowl.

"Can I get a five-egg omelet with onions and cheese, some pancakes, and a couple of cartons of orange juice?"

"Sure! I'm working on a new recipe for the omelets. Wanna try spinach and feta?"

I shrug. I'm starving. I'll eat just about anything right now.

The pancakes come out first, and I wolf them down. He's got a little grin on his face as he pushes the omelet across the counter. It smells delicious, like butter and caramelized onion. There're green flecks sprinkled over it. But it's the only thing on the plate.

"Hey, last year, Toby always added home fries and toast. Can I get those?"

He arches an eyebrow. "Sure." He pulls bread from a bag as he talks to me, then scoops potatoes onto the flat-top grill. He knows where everything is without looking for it. He doesn't take a step, and yet, less than a minute later, he serves me four pieces of perfectly buttered toast and a heap of home fries, studded with garlic.

"Sorry. I thought you wanted pancakes *instead* of toast."

There's something familiar about his eyes. I guess I should ask his name, but I'm still eating. The home fries taste amazing. Instead of mentioning it to him I mentally replay that last split. My breathing was off. I'll ask Koji tonight.

After I finish, I go to the locker room to shower and change into my uniform. I sign in at the front desk, avoid Raheem, the manager, and check my texts. The pool opens at 9:30. Mirrored aviators in place, I'm on the lifeguard stand when I see the whiteboard through the snack bar window. He must have written on it while I was inside. My name is in bright green letters.

"Special Today: Basil Rickey! Like lime and mint, only BETTER!"

I'm so pissed I almost jump off the guard stand. I *never* agreed to let the pool use me to sell food. But there are kids in the water, and I can't leave. I stare at the sign, furious, for the next twenty-eight minutes. I have to barter lifeguard time for free pool use; it's the only way to get enough time in the water. When I worked all of this out with the pool manager last summer, he never said anything about UCSC using me as an advertising ploy. I don't know anyone here other than the team and I'm not interested in making friends. Our old home in Manchester is over an hour away. That was the best part about working here. I could practice without people knowing who I was and bothering me—until now. And with the Submergd contract it will only get worse. *Goddammit.*

I just want to swim. I want to swim faster and better than I did yesterday. I don't want to pose for magazine pictures in a Submergd swimsuit. I don't want to call Mr. Taplin. I don't want to nod and smile when people compare me to that other swimmer, the one who first qualified for the Olympics at age fifteen, the one who has twenty-eight medals, more medals than any other Olympian, in any sport, ever. And I definitely do not want to be this summer's Upper Collingford Swim Club celebrity mascot.

The second it's ten o'clock, I blow my whistle to announce adult swim. Kids whine and complain, but straggle out of the pool and, as three adults calmly swim laps, I seize my chance.

I'm at the snack bar window in seconds. The cook gives me a big grin. "Hungry again already?"

"What the fuck is a Basil Rickey?"

My tone startles him. "It's today's special, a drink. I'll make you one. I think you'll like it. You can help me figure out how many limes to—"

"Take my name off it."

"Your what?" He turns away, pitcher in hand. He actually pretends he doesn't know what he's done.

"Take. My. Name. Off. It. I train here. I work as a lifeguard. I get free food when I'm on duty. I'm nice to people when they want an autograph or a selfie. That's the deal. I'm not pitching products for you. I'm not for sale."

Whoever-he-is puts the pitcher down, calmly turns back to me, and leans against the counter. The grin is gone. One taut forearm has a tattoo of a whisk. We glare at each other, and I remember where I know him from.

"You're Toby's younger brother. He brought you to work a couple of times last year."

"Yeah, I'm Will. And you're an asshole."

Will

"Toby, what's with that swimmer, Basil?"

"You mean The Orca? He's an aquatic predator—swims fast, stays in the water, kills his competition, and eats everything in his path. What happened?"

"He told me I can't serve my new drink because it has basil in it."

"What did you say?"

"I called him out, and he stormed off. Why is he such a douche?"

"Dunno. I just fed him—more crap than you can believe. I didn't get a lot of thanks or any tips, just more orders. You can forget setting your sights on him, dude, he doesn't have any friends, let alone *romantic* interests. He's all swimming and eating."

I pocket my phone, a little less confused but still pissed off. I stare at the pool from the counter of the snack bar. This was supposed to be a fun summer job, taking over the snack bar from Toby, who's spending the summer at a tony private school to make up for his crappy grades. I was supposed to get to watch for hot swimmers, earn minimum wage plus tips, and show off my cooking chops. Instead, I'm playing waiter to some jock who thinks everything's about him, including my first fabulous culinary innovation.

"Did you make a drink about The Orca?"

It's Keisha, one of the senior-team swimmers, smiling and dripping. Before I can answer, she laughs and says, "I'll take one, but he's not going to like it."

"I made an awesome drink out of basil because my mother's garden exploded early this year. Thank you, global warming." I pour the basil syrup over crushed ice. "Nothing to do with *that* guy."

She takes a sip. "Yum." She turns to her friends, who are sitting on the edge of the pool. "You guys, try this."

That's how my first lunchtime rush starts. Toby said it would be quiet, people trickling in, getting a hot dog here, fries there. But a whole group comes over. They order rickeys, and Keisha says, "Pics or it didn't happen!" She takes a group selfie with everyone holding up their green drinks. She posts it on Instagram, invites me to follow her, and says to her friends, "Thirsty, Orca?" That cracks them up. This is great!

They like the rickeys so much that they ask me what else I have. I sell out of feta and spinach omelets in minutes.

"Have you got anything else?"

Nothing, but I think fast. "Come back for a new special every day. But I'm guessing you haven't tried hot dogs as good as mine." Those sell out, too, and I thank whatever divine being invented clarified butter.

"You should be a chef when you graduate!"

Suh-weet! It's as if they know who I am from eating my food. "I'm gonna be." I want to be one of those chefs who creates new flavor combos that people taste then wonder why no one did it before. I'll go on TV and win contests, like the one on *Cookd*, start my own restaurant, feed people. This is the beginning.

Even Basil comes over again, alone, of course. His thick, dark hair is cropped short without a part. It would be black, but all that time in the pool makes it very dark gray instead. His eyes are dark, too, brown, with long lashes. He doesn't order a rickey—big surprise.

He looks at the whiteboard again, rolls his eyes, frowns, and growls, "Two cheeseburgers, two hot dogs, and a double order of fries."

I ignore him while I prepare his food and resist the urge to spit on it. He takes the tray without a word.

When the lunch rush dies down, and I'm picking up the plates and napkins from the four tables in front of the counter, I realize what I've done suggesting daily specials. How am I going to come up with new specials every day this summer? That's like seventy-five days, and I only have snack bar equipment: flat-top, deep fryer, and a soft-serve machine. Then there's the problem of ingredients. Raheem doesn't understand anything but burgers, dogs, and fries. He's the first one I need to sell on new stuff. Time for some esculent prestidigitation, I guess.

I check the clock: 2:00 p.m., three hours to go, and it's dead. What can I serve after lunch to bring people in? Nothing too filling, so smallish stuff. Snacks, but better than just the bags of chips on the rack.

"Hey, Willie, I need to talk to you."

"Sure, Raheem, what is it?" I hate being called "Willie," but don't correct him. This is my chance to negotiate for ingredients.

"What did you do to piss off the swimming champ?"

Uh oh. "Um, nothing."

"He says you're using his name on a drink. He's pissed."

"No! I made a drink with basil, not a drink named, 'Basil.'" He told my boss? What an asshole! "I sold out, two dozen between eleven-thirty and now."

"Well, no more basil drinks. Basil Minopoli is training for the Olympics. It's good for the club that he practices here—prestigious."

"Okay, Raheem, no more basil rickeys, promise."

"You gotta feed that guy what he wants."

"What do you mean?"

"He gets to eat whatever he wants and he wants a ton of food every day. It's a swimming thing. He basically eats all the summer profits from this snack bar. But the good PR's worth it."

Hmmm. "Sure thing, Raheem."

"We gotta keep him happy. Just burgers, dogs, fries. You cook fancier stuff on your own time. Don't give him any lip either."

I wipe down the whiteboard thinking that I'd like to wipe Basil's face right off his head, starting with *his* lip.

Although, thinking about his full lips, I might wipe off the rest of his face and leave his mouth where it is. Oh, and the big, dark eyes, too, long lashes and all.

*   *   *

BASIL STANDS SCOWLING OUTSIDE THE snack bar the next morning when I raise the metal shade. His eyes dart to the whiteboard over my shoulder. I haven't put up today's special yet. He relaxes his scowl to a simple frown. *What a prince.*

"I want six eggs, scrambled, hash browns, whole wheat toast, and a short stack."

Ignoring his omission of the word "please," I smile. "Sorry," *not sorry,* "no eggs. They haven't come yet."

"Seriously? I need the protein. When are they coming?"

"Dunno. We're out of hash browns, too. Double up on the toast?"

"No. Make it fries instead. Do you have cheese fries?"

"Sorry," *not sorry.* "It'll take half an hour to heat up the fryolater. How about grilled cheese?"

"Is that all you got?"

"I could put bacon on it."

"Okay. Three and double up on the pancakes." He juts out his lower lip.

Yeah, I wouldn't wipe that off.

He watches me as I work. I'm itching to put today's special on the whiteboard, but I hold off.

He doesn't thank me when I hand him his tray. He takes it to a table and demolishes everything. Toby's wrong: He's not a killer whale: He's one of those whales that just opens its mouth and sucks everything in. Good thing I didn't waste today's special on him.

Here's the thing: My mom's garden *did* explode with basil—lower case b—and it's such a great summer flavor that I *have* to use it. So if Basil wants his protein, I'm going to offer it with his favorite herb. I just won't name it. I grab the step stool and the markers and write on the whiteboard, "Special Today: Pesto Tuna Melt, a Summer Breeze that's Genoese."

When he's through eating, Basil tips his tray into the trash bin, then leaves it on top. But there's still trash on his table, the slob. He heads to the locker room without even looking at me. *You're welcome, Basil. Swim good.*

It's still quiet, so I step out and pick up his stupid trash: one of those wrappers, paper on the outside, foil on the inside. *Strawberry Milkshake Pop-Tart? Gross.*

Back behind the counter, I open the fridge and grin at the eggs in their open crate.

Basil lifeguards for an hour, so doesn't see the golden hash browns I dish up. Everyone loves them. When lunch rolls around I sell fifteen pesto tuna melts, saving a couple of scoops of the tuna salad just in case.

"What's pesto tuna?" I don't even need to look up to know it's him by the total lack of manners, no hello, nothing.

"Oh, it's great, very summery. Tuna salad with pesto sauce—"

"—and pesto sauce is full of—"

"Do you want one?"

"Three burgers and three hot dogs. Did you get your fryo-thing hot?"

"I'm down to one burger and, yes, we've got fries."

"Okay, one burger, three dogs, fries, and two of your tuna sandwiches."

Sweeeeet!

BASIL

IT TAKES ME A FEW days to realize what Will is doing. Every morning there's a new special with basil in it on his whiteboard. He stops using my name, but the day after the tuna with pesto he offers a Grilled Cheese Caprese Sandwich—All the Colors of the Italian Flag. The next day it's a Green Hummus Veggie Pita, and then Garlic Breadsticks with Herb Butter. Yeah, he's trolling me.

But why? It's not as though we had any kind of argument. When he called me an asshole the first day, I just walked away. I know when someone's trying to start a fight and I'm not taking the bait. I could text Toby—we were sort of friends last year—but I should call Mr. Taplin first.

Yesterday, I hit the wall wrong in a turn and bruised my left foot. Koji's not happy. We have a team meet next week, and my times are all off. This morning I get to the pool at 4:00 a.m. to ice my foot before my solo practice.

Koji arrives at 4:30.

"Arm crawl today if that foot's still a problem." He tosses me a kickboard to hold between my knees. It's Koji's way of giving me a break. I decide to ask him.

"Any idea why that cook, Will, is mad at me?"

"Maybe you eat too much."

"Real funny. No, seriously. He's put basil in his special every day this week. I think he's making fun of me."

"You just described a third-grade crush, not a fight. You want me to talk to Raheem? That kid needs to feed you."

"No, he's feeding me, but he's—"

"Quit thinking about some cook with big blue eyes. You should be focused on not hitting the goddamn wall like you're in a kiddy pool."

At 4:40, I finish my second Pop-Tart on my way from the locker room to the pool. It's still dark outside but there's a light in the snack bar. Will is writing on a clipboard while a huge pot of water simmers on the cooktop. There's a giant pile of sliced onions and garlic on the counter and some sort of steak. He's concentrating hard. Something about the look on his face makes me stop at the door.

"Why are you here so early?" It startles him.

"I get here early to order supplies and do prep work."

"Don't you just cook what people order?"

He cocks his head at me as if I've just said something stupid.

"Do you really think I can cook eggs, bacon, hash browns, and pancakes in under a minute? Everything has to be out and ready to go before anyone gets here. I pre-cook the bacon, chop onions and garlic, mix pancake batter. It's called *mise en place*. Then, when you place an order, all I do is measure out portions and fry."

There's an angry red mark on the back of his wrist. "That must hurt."

He shrugs. I'm about to ask more when Koji calls. 4:46. I'm late again.

By the end of practice, my foot is killing me. Will opens his window as I limp toward the counter.

"Need some ice?"

I slump onto a chair and nod. Will brings a bag, which I press against my ankle. The cold makes me wince. He's so close I can smell garlic and lemons.

"Thanks. Did you save some for your wrist?"

He gives me a smile—almost—before heading back to the kitchen. A few minutes later he comes back with a plate of scrambled eggs, bacon, half a cantaloupe, and a huge pile of hash browns. He has two apple juice bottles under his arm. He puts it all on the table in front of me. For the first time in my life, I inspect the hash browns before I eat them. They have a crisp brown crust and they smell oniony.

"They're awesome."

"True. Why are you practicing if your foot is hurt?"

"Something is always hurt. That doesn't give me an excuse. We have a meet next week."

This is the first real conversation we've had.

"What event do you swim?"

"IM—individual medley. It's four lengths, with four different strokes: butterfly, back, breast, and free."

There's an awkward silence, but he asked me about swimming, so I ask him about cooking. "What's the special today?"

"I'm still deciding."

"I saw the steak you had out earlier."

"It's flank steak."

"That sounds good."

"It's not on the menu."

"How come?"

"I don't have the budget to serve that cut of steak to everyone. I come in early so I can practice dishes like that."

"You practice cooking?"

"How else am I going to get better?"

"How exactly do you practice on a steak?"

My phone buzzes: Leo Taplin. *Shit.* I never did call him. I answer the phone to get it over with.

"Hey, Basil, we'll be out with a film crew next week to get some practice shots. Wednesday work for you?"

"Uhhh, there's a meet on Thursday, so I don't think—"

"Perfect. We need tape of you swimming, and warming up, and anything else that you do as part of your routine. We can talk about the *Wake-Up America* spot. Everyone's excited to have you on board. We have a new line of suits. Michael Phelps helped design them. Can't wait to see if you like them."

"I can't—" He's gone. *Shit.* But there's nothing I can do except what he says.

Will's still here, watching me. His eyes are more gray than blue this morning. I wish Koji hadn't mentioned them.

After practice, the whiteboard says that today's special is Turkey BLT with Zucchini Fries—no basil. But that's not what Will feeds me. Instead, he pushes a plate across the counter with the grilled flank steak, white sauce oozing out of it, and a mountain of sweet potato fries next to it.

"Tell me what it needs."

My mouth is already full. He stands there watching while I eat half the steak and most of the fries. I take a swig of water.

"I think it's great."

"Maybe roasted red pepper in the goat cheese stuffing?"

"Sure, I guess."

"Or mashed potatoes instead of fried sweets?"

"If you wanted."

"It's not what *I* want. That's not how cooking works. It's what the diner wants. Everybody has their own taste. Some people like orange instead of lemon. Some people hate coconut—the idiots—and you can never, ever convince them to eat it. Some people love junk food." Usually I follow the schedule, follow Koji's instructions, follow Submergd's rules. But Will really wants to know what I like. It's so unexpected I don't know how to answer.

"Maybe a bigger steak?"

He laughs, and yeah, his eyes turn from gray back to blue.

"Hey, if you need some certain kind of food after practice, just ask me. I can add stuff to the list. I don't know what swimmers eat, but—"

"Can you do something with bananas?"

"Sure. Why?"

"The potassium. I like to load up before a meet. It might help my foot also."

"What did you do to your foot?"

"Koji made me do splits without goggles. I mistimed a turn."

"Why? Isn't the point to see where you're going so you don't crash into a wall?"

"No, the point is to know the pool so well that, even if you lose your goggles in a race, it won't stop you. I know when to turn because I know when to turn, not because I see the marker."

"So *mise en place*, but underwater."

Before I can answer, Koji comes up behind me. He's about to leave for the day. "No more resting that foot; we need to get on it, Basil. See you tonight."

Will pulls my empty plate back. "You have a nice day too," he says to Koji's back. He catches me stifling a laugh and smirks.

WILL

OKAY, THIS GUY'S A CHALLENGE. He eats the steak, but doesn't taste the sizzle. When they are interviewed on *Cookd*, the contestants always talk about strategy: understanding what the judges like and how to get them interested. Here at *Chez* UCSC, I've got the crowd—I sell out of my specials and most of the other stuff— but I can't get the judge. I stopped tweaking him by slipping his namesake herb into everything. He definitely noticed, because his sour puss disappeared with the basil and now he puzzles over the specials every day with a towel over his broad shoulder and water pooling at his long feet. Then he orders everything.

[To Toby] He's not a jerk anymore. He just doesn't notice what I serve.

[To Will] Yeah. And the problem is?

[To Toby] IDK. I'm killing myself trying to get some attention, and he doesn't care.

[To Will] Told you—no romantic interest!

Huh? I respond to the little pink hearts in Toby's text with a middle finger emoji. But maybe he's right. What do I care? I guess it's more than the challenge of getting him to notice my food. There are those lips, after all, and those dark eyes, focused on my burned wrist.

Basil obviously likes volume. He goes for huge amounts of protein at every meal and doesn't skimp on the carbs. He likes rich and heavy too. He has no interest in salads, didn't want the zucchini fries, and turned down the hummus. He inhales his food without pausing between bites. I either need to slow him down or surprise him.

I try using swimming terms I find online. He orders a "Shrimp Po'Buoy" along with his burgers and dogs but doesn't notice the spelling. Nor does he slow down to eat it or tell me he likes it—a total waste of the delectable remoulade, if I do say so myself. He doesn't even order the "PB & J French Toast" I offer, despite the description of "Protein, Fruit, and Carbs, Together at Last!"

Today, at the end of lunchtime, he comes by as usual, but only asks for a couple of bottles of water.

"Nothing to eat?"

"No."

"How come?"

"Some guy is coming by to interview me about swimming."

"You're usually starved right now. I have a Slider Medley today, four different mini-burgers."

"Just water," he snaps.

Return of the sour puss!

It turns out the "guy" is two guys and a camera crew. First, they take a bunch of shots of Basil diving into the pool, swimming laps, and doing flip turns. Then they push a table and chairs away from the snack bar counter toward the wall of the club building and plug in some super-bright lights, which they train on Basil. He towels off, looking in my direction. He must be starving, but they aren't finished.

Basil may be a swimming champ but he's no smooth celebrity. He sits as though he's in the electric chair waiting for someone to throw the switch. The lights glint from his bugged-out eyes. A makeup guy leans over him, but Basil recoils. One of the guys, who must be the Submergd rep, gives him a new tank top to wear—Basil must already have a closet full of that stuff—then one of the camera crew puts a big white makeup bib on it. Basil can hardly hold still. He twists his hands and clenches his jaw. Do they really need makeup? He's got that olive skin, glowing and flawless.

After they put the makeup on Basil and strip off the bib, Koji comes by in a Submergd windbreaker. He wants to sit at the table, but Submergd Guy tells him to step back while they're filming.

Mike Corrente, the anchor from National Sports Network, sits facing Basil and smiles. Basil looks down and clutches his water bottle for all he's worth. Corrente asks Basil where he grew up (Manchester), how many siblings he has (sister), and how it feels to be a potential Olympian (fine). Basil gives one-word answers without making eye contact. I can't take my eyes off the scene. It's like a slow-motion car crash.

Koji stands back by the camera waving both arms at Basil, trying to animate him. Submergd Guy bends to say something in Basil's ear.

Corrente tries again.

"So Basil, you must be familiar with the most famous Olympic swimmer, Michael Phelps. Has he inspired you in some way?"

Basil grips the water bottle so hard that I'm positive it's going to explode. The crew eye each other. But Basil's not angry. He's scared.

I get an idea. I take out some bananas and start cutting. I throw some bittersweet chocolate in the microwave. While that's heating, I work the soft-serve machine. In three minutes, I load a tray which I bring to the table where Mike Corrente and Basil are gaping at each other. The cameras are still rolling.

"Splits for the swimmer! Banana splits, that is." I make a big flourish of putting two bowls on the table. Is that relief I see on Basil's face? I don't stay to find out. The cameraman puts down his camera, so I offer the rest of the banana splits to the crew. Koji declines with a snarl.

"Hey, kid, this is good with the nuts and all." It's Corrente. "Come over here." He stands up when I return to the table. "Are you the star's private chef?"

"I'm the star!" I blurt out without thinking. "I mean, I'm the star of the kitchen, while Basil is the star of the water!"

"Sit down with us. Tell me how you know Basil." He gestures to the crew, who come over with a chair and makeup.

I look at Basil to see if he minds. He shrugs. No, he shrugs and nods. He wants me to sit down. I hold still while they make up my face and turn the cameras back on.

"I'm sitting here with Basil Minopoli and his friend…"

"Will Crane."

"…Will Crane. For the very few who don't know him yet, Basil is headed to the next Summer Olympics. He trains every day here at the Upper Collingford Swim Club, where Will runs the kitchen. How did you guys meet?"

Basil turns to me, his eyes wide.

"Well, Mike, swimmers eat a ton of food every day, and my Olympic sport is producing that ton of food for Basil." *I can't believe I'm being this corny.* "I serve Basil the standard snack bar stuff, but sometimes he requests certain ingredients, like the bananas in these banana splits."

Basil nods. "I need the potassium before a meet." It's his first full sentence on camera. I catch myself staring at his mouth again.

"He also lets me try out my real gustatory exploits after hours."

Corrente chuckles. "Basil, do you have a favorite food that Will cooks?"

"Um, sure. He made a, a flank steak stuffed with goat cheese and herbs the other night. It was off-menu. I could've eaten three of them."

Sweet! He noticed, and now my dish is going to be on national television!

"That's great. I hope you get at least two more steaks very soon. Will, we'll let you get back to work while we talk swimming with your athlete here." He nods, dismissing me. Basil passes over his empty bowl with a silent "thanks."

There are more questions, but they obviously don't want me here. I glance at Basil but can't read his face.

I clean up and prepare to shut down for the day. If they finish up with Basil and he wants something, I can make it, but no one else is coming by at this hour. A sharp knock on the closed metal curtain over the counter startles me. It's Koji.

"No more ice cream socials. You got that?"

"Huh?"

"Stick to your work and stay away from my guy. He needs to focus on his swimming, not on some burger flipper who thinks he's gonna be the next Gordon Ramsay."

BASIL

AS SOON AS MIKE CORRENTE leaves, I head for Will. The screen is down, but he's inside cleaning the grill. All the food is put away, except for one pot on the cooktop. My stomach growls.

"Hey, those banana splits were good. Have you got anything else? Even some peanut butter crackers? I'm really hungry and that was really... awful."

Will leans down to pick up a dropped rag. The muscles in his forearm flex, stirring his whisk tattoo.

"Let me see what I've got." He smiles. "You'll settle for peanut butter?"

"Yeah, I'm done for the day. I love peanut butter. I could eat it every night."

"What was awful, the interview?"

"Mr. Taplin wants to do a whole series for *Wake-Up America*. You saw how bad it went. I'm going to look like a total douche on morning TV."

"No one watches morning TV," he assures me, holding out an industrial-size jar of peanut butter and a box of saltines. I dig in while he opens a large can of tuna and puts four slices of bread in the toaster. I lean against the doorjamb to watch. He doesn't look as he pulls out the stuff—*mise en place.*

The sandwich is delicious. Instead of mayonnaise, he used the same sauce that he put on the shrimp the other day. He grins when I ask him about it. As I eat the last bite he turns to the stove and ladles out something onto two rolls.

"Chili dogs?"

I didn't even see him heat the hot dogs. I wolf one down, still hungry. The chili tastes warm, different somehow. I can't place it.

"I wish you could do the interviews for me. You were so much better on camera."

"Too bad Submergd doesn't sponsor chefs. Someday, when I get my own cooking show. Anyway, I knew you were starving and figured some food would loosen things up."

He leans against the counter and watches me eat. His eyes are mixed blue-gray today.

"Try pretending the cameras aren't there. Also, eat before you start. Then you can concentrate on answering questions without wanting to gnaw your hand off."

Not ravenous anymore, I bite into the second chili dog. I think I figured out the taste. "Is it cinnamon?"

"Yes! It mellows the heat of the peppers. You do notice what I feed you." He grins again.

My phone buzzes with two texts. The first is from Mr. Taplin.

Ask your friend Will for another swimming-themed dish tomorrow. We want footage with him for a segment on your training regimen.

I shove the phone at Will so he can read the text. "Guess you were wrong. Submergd wants you back on camera. You can save my ass again—and show off your cooking."

His eyes widen, then he wipes his hands on his apron and pulls the pen out of his sleeve pocket.

"I need to make a menu and a shopping list. This is huge. I owe you."

The second text is from Mom, held up at work so she can't come get me. I still haven't had time to take my driver's test.

"Any way you can pay me back with a ride home? I have to shower and change, but there's no evening practice because of the meet tomorrow. My mom's running late."

Will's buried in the refrigerator, list in hand, but he gives me a thumbs-up over his shoulder.

In the locker room, Koji asks about my left bicep, which was bothering me earlier. I tell him about Mr. Taplin's invitation.

"Start focusing, stop flirting."

"I'm not flirting. Will just makes me… calmer. You saw how bad I was today. The only good part of that interview was when he came in."

"You know what you need to do against Rivera and Danielson. Scott's the wild card tomorrow." Jay Scott just moved to Greenwich, Connecticut from Oklahoma. He's put up some fast numbers in the IM, and I've watched him on tape, but this is our first race against each other.

Will comes in from the kitchen, twirling his car keys on a finger. Koji grabs my arm.

"You've got too many distractions right now, Basil. This isn't how you prepare for a race. You're going to regret this."

"The bicep is fine. I'll see you tomorrow."

He stalks off without looking at Will, who blows a kiss at Koji's back. It shouldn't make me laugh but it does.

In the car, I connect my pre-race playlist to Will's stereo. He smirks when Free Boyz starts.

"Rap from when we were in middle school?"

"I picked it when I started racing four years ago. You don't mess with the pre-race ritual."

"Are swimmers superstitious? Got any other good luck rituals?"

I tell him about only using white towels and always stretching on the right side first, then ask him about cooking to change the subject. He got his mom to buy him half a pig when he was twelve so he could learn how to butcher it. My entire playlist appalls him. As he pulls into my neighborhood, I realize that Koji would call this flirting, but this is the most relaxed I've been before a race since, well, maybe ever. Will's easy to talk to. My arm isn't twinging as much, and I'm not that nervous about tomorrow since Will is going to be there.

"What's with the Pop-Tarts?"

"What do you mean?" *How did he find out?*

"I pick up your trash. Why do you eat Strawberry Milkshake Pop-Tarts every morning? They're barely food. I'm asking as your new personal chef."

I've never told anyone about this, not even my parents. They probably think it's another weird habit. We're in my driveway now, and I could tell him I need to leave, but I don't. I finger the door handle as I talk.

"My grandfather is the one who made me and my sister learn how to swim. His younger brother drowned back in Crete when they were kids. I'm named after him. Pappou brought us to the pool every day after Greek School for swimming lessons. Afterward, he bought us strawberry milkshakes at the snack bar."

"Okay, healthy, dairy, fruit. Why did you switch to the hydrogenated version?"

"Pappou died the month before my first big race when I was thirteen. He didn't care about racing, but he wanted to cheer me on. Right after the funeral I saw a box of Strawberry Milkshake Pop-Tarts in the store. They… they just reminded me of him. It was as if he was sending me a message. I took two Pop-Tarts with me to the race and won with a fast-enough time that Koji noticed, and he talked to my parents about coaching me. So now—"

Will touches my arm. "So now you don't mess with the pre-race ritual." His hand is warm.

*   *   *

MOST SWIMMERS SHAVE THE DAY before a race, but I do it the day of. I get to the Club at 6:02 a.m. and take a long shower, mentally rehearsing each split of the relay, removing every hair from my legs, my arms, my torso.

I've eaten a couple of bananas and today's Pop-Tarts, but I need more food. Will is making something special with a swimming theme. Funny how much I look forward to what he cooks, not only because I'm always hungry, but because he's excited about cooking for me. Koji was wrong. I'm loose, focused, and ready. On the deck, I catch Will sneaking a glance at me as I pull a Submergd warm-up jacket over my newly smooth chest.

Koji tells Mr. Taplin they have five minutes of camera time now but need to wait until after I race for more. Mike Corrente isn't here today, so Mr. Taplin asks the questions. I'm in a chair next to him, and the camera man is filming. Jay Scott's coach watches from the far side of the deck, but I'm not nervous. I focus on Will instead of the cameras, and it works. I can do this. Koji was wrong.

Mr. Taplin asks how I warm up, and I explain some of my stretches, but not all of them. Too much information gives people like Jay Scott a chance to mess with my head. Still, no problems, way better than yesterday. Koji nods at me from behind the camera. When Mr. Taplin asks about what I eat before a race, Will brings over a plate and hands it to me. The yellow stacks on it look like pancakes and smell buttery.

I dig in as he explains to Mr. Taplin that he's created a new race day dish for me, with carbs and proteins. Mr. Taplin loves it.

And suddenly it all goes bad—very, very bad.

My mouth is full as Will proudly announces that I'm eating Freestyle Breakfast Arepas, corncakes with eggs on top, stuffed with bananas and peanut butter.

I don't stop to think. The camera catches me spitting out a half-chewed mouthful. I drop the plate, which smashes on the concrete deck, and sprint for the locker room. Mr. Taplin calls after me but I don't stop. I need to wash my mouth out *right now*.

Will is behind his counter when I get back to the deck. He won't look in my direction. Koji won't let me go talk to him. I argue, but he shakes his head and nods to Jay Scott, who stares at us from the other side of the pool. Koji sends me off to the locker room to stretch and run my playlist. An hour later, I receive a text from Mr. Taplin asking to meet with my parents next week about whether I'm still a good fit for Submergd.

Jay Scott beats me in the IM by four hundredths of a second.

WILL

WTF!

After dropping Basil off last night, I went to Whole Trader's and made up the recipe on my phone before going inside. No way was I going to risk the standard Northeast Restaurant Supply ingredients for Basil's meet. I got the best peanut butter, because he said he could eat it every night. I got cornmeal and fresh corn to make the arepas beautiful, soft and sweet, to provide on-demand energy from the carbs. I roasted bananas, caramelizing them just enough to bring out some smoke, knowing he needs the potassium. Uncured, apple-smoked bacon gave the whole thing crunch, and fried eggs supplied extra protein without being heavy. I spent a ton of my own money getting all organic stuff— no wonder my mother calls the store "Whole Paycheck." But I figured it was worth it to make something this piquant, since I'd be on TV as Basil's personal chef.

But he goes and spits it out—on camera—then runs away and doesn't even thank me!

No one has to say "cut" for me to know the filming's finished, and I make a hasty exit. Taplin and his crew stay around for some of the meet, but I don't watch. I wipe the "Freestyle Breakfast Arepas" off the whiteboard and leave it blank. Screw everyone. I put away the bananas and the arepa batter. No one's going to want something a star athlete spit out.

I don't have time to think about it because there are so many people here to watch the meet that I can't get the food out fast enough. It'll quiet down later. This late in July, all the schoolkids are in day camp, so there's no family crowd on weekdays, just the lane swimmers who never order anything and the old people who rave about my iced tea but cluck about the price of the hot dogs. Business will be quiet this afternoon.

The meet's over by lunchtime, and the teams pack up. I'm wrong about it quieting down here, though. Keisha comes over with a bunch of her teammates.

"Hey, Will, no special today?"

I shrug. "Nothing anyone would want."

Keisha grins. "Oh, come on, we saw you bring something to The Orca. Just 'cause we're not on TV you're not going to give it to us?"

"Didn't you see him spit it out?"

"Whatevs. He's a nutter. He probably forgot to say the right prayer before eating. He lost his race anyway. At least tell us what it was."

I bristle when she insults Basil. Then I feel bad that he lost his race, with the Submergd people there and all. But I catch myself. There was nothing wrong with my arepas. I pull out the batter and the bananas.

Keisha and her friends prove me right. "Next meet here, you have to make this for us. It's the perfect breakfast!"

Sweet.

Within half an hour, I sell out and mentally add up the sales. I'm cleaning up the lunch stuff when Koji and Basil come to the counter. There are no niceties. Basil looks away while Koji orders. "Three burgers, three dogs, two fries, and some orange juice."

When I ask Basil how the meet went, Koji steps between us to block me. "Leave him alone. Stay in your lane."

Basil still won't look at me when I hand Koji the tray. They take it to a table in front of the snack bar. The place is almost empty. Keisha left with her friends fifteen minutes ago.

"What the hell was that?" Koji starts in, loud enough that I can hear from behind the counter.

"Dunno. Sorry."

"Your start was bad. You were sloppy on the splits and you didn't push the finish. Not to mention you made a mess with Submergd on camera."

"I didn't—"

"You didn't listen to me. I told you to stay away. That snack bar whiz doesn't give a rat's ass about you or your swimming. He's after the television coverage only. He's ruining your focus."

"Yeah, I guess."

That's all I need to hear. This kitchen is closed. I carefully pull down the metal screen so they don't think I care and finish cleaning up. If that's what Basil-the-swimmer thinks, he can forget peanut butter, bananas, and anything without basil-the-herb in it.

*   *   *

I catch all kinds of hell the next morning. Raheem, who usually doesn't appear before 9:00 a.m., stands waiting for me when I arrive with his arms crossed and a big frown bisecting his face.

"Give me one good reason why I shouldn't fire your ass."

"Um." I keep my eyes level with his, hoping he doesn't see the bunch of green leaves sticking out of my canvas bag. He won't care about the bread and tomatoes. Those could be for grilled cheese.

"What did I tell you about that swimming star?"

"I, uh—"

"What did I tell you about all this fancy food?"

"Sorry."

"Didn't I say burgers-dogs-fries, whatever else he wants and however much?"

"Yuh."

"I haven't run the numbers for July yet, since we're only half-way through, but we can't break even feeding that guy and there's no way we can afford to lose money on all that fancy crap you're making. I can't believe he asked for 'Freestyle Arepas.'"

"It won't—"

"It better not."

"The gross has been—"

"Don't tell me about the gross. You made our Olympic contender barf on camera. Now he's gonna lose his sponsorship and Upper Collingford is gonna look terrible, all because some Ottolenghi wannabe can't keep his face away from the cameras."

I'm too surprised that he knows who Yotam Ottolenghi is to explain that I bought all the ingredients for the arepas myself and that the Snack Bar is doing fifty percent better than it did last year. He'd know it himself if he could work the POS system.

"I don't care how hard it is to replace you mid-summer. If I hear one more complaint, Crane, you're out!" He storms off without waiting for me to respond.

I want to yell back at Raheem that I'm trying to cook what Basil wants but with Koji barking at me and Basil avoiding me, I can't even ask.

I hear Basil come in, but the screen's down and he doesn't poke his head in the side door. That's fine with me. He can apologize when he's ready but the longer he takes, the less I'm likely to listen.

When I pull the screen up to open, I find myself face-to-face with Koji again. Basil sits at one of the tables, his back to me.

"Three eggs, over, sausage, pancakes, toast, hash, and OJ. No gourmet crap."

"Coming right up."

Two can play this game. Well, maybe three if you count Basil. Ordinarily, if he sat down at a table before I had the food ready, I'd step out and bring the tray over, but not today.

"Food's up." I slam the tray on the counter and keep my back turned until I hear one of them come get it. Too bad the toast is burned.

"So we're clear, the only blue you pay attention to is the water, not some camera-hogging poser's eyes."

Basil's tone is subdued. "I know."

I can't close, so I turn back to the whiteboard and write up the special, "Open-faced Bruschetta Sandwich: All the Flavors of Summer!"

BASIL

FOR THE FIRST TIME IN my life, I'm not hungry.

I still need food though. Whatever Koji brings me, I eat mechanically. I wake up at 4:15 a.m., I get to practice on time, I do whatever Koji tells me without question. But my times are off, my starts are weak, and the throbbing in my right hamstring won't go away.

I don't know what to say to Will so I don't say anything. The only thing I do is follow orders.

The meeting with Submergd is bad. Mr. Taplin tells my parents that I'm not "aligned with the gear" in a way that will showcase either my talents or the company's interests. Dad is perplexed, Mom is upset, and none of us knows how we can pay Koji's fees. All these years of training, all the early morning practices, and now, no matter how fast I swim, the Olympics are out because I don't know how to act for a camera.

Koji says Submergd is in talks with Jay Scott.

The first race I won—the one after Pappou died—Koji talked to my parents for a long time while I showered and changed. When I came back, he took us for lunch at the Miss Manchester Diner. I wolfed down waffles and sausage while he explained what he saw in me. I was tall for thirteen and flexible, but what he was most interested in was that I didn't joke around with the rest of the team.

"You don't need to be unfriendly," he explained to me. "Carry yourself apart, focus on your own practice and on your own times. That's the difference between excellent swimmers and Michael Phelps." The only reason I thought I could swim the same times as an Olympic legend was because Koji said I could.

For three years, it's worked. All the comparisons to Him from all sorts of people fed my superstitions. My family knows not to say His name. When outsiders notice that we're the same height or that I'm only a year older than He was when He first qualified for the Sydney Olympics, I change the subject, then get back in the pool. From the time Koji told me I could be the best, that's all I've focused on doing. I've followed all of Koji's orders and I've gotten better and better. Until now.

Until Will.

I lose in the next meet when I swim against Antonio Rivera. My IM time slips another two hundredths of a second. The rest of the team crowds around the snack bar afterward, eating and laughing with Will. I head for the locker room.

Koji takes me out for lunch, away from the club. I pick at a Reuben while he watches.

"You're supposed to eat it, not pull it apart like a Lego set. Do you want something else?"

I shrug and force a mouthful down.

"Basil, talk to me. What's going on? Is it the hamstring? We can get an appointment with Dr. Olowe."

"I'm not hungry."

"Yes, you are. You just raced."

"The sandwich is cold."

He orders me a ham and Swiss omelet.

"If I can't get Submergd back we can't afford you."

"And you know I want to keep coaching you. But I have to pay the bills too. You know what to do, Basil."

"I can't—"

"Listen, Basil, I know you hate being compared to high-performing athletes, but you shouldn't. They all have one thing in common: total focus. You come to practice, you do the work, you put in the hours, and you have the right body morph. With all that, you should be going to the Games. Maybe not Tokyo, but maybe Paris. Or Los Angeles in '28. Maybe all of them. But not if you let this guy distract you. It's your decision, not mine, but you better make it. You need a coach. I need a paycheck. You need to adjust."

"So I'm not supposed to have friends? I'm not supposed to ever like a guy? I'm supposed to do nothing but swim laps and practice starts until 2028?"

He flips a couple of twenties on the table and pushes back his chair.

"You know what to do. Do it and you'll win again. You don't adjust, well, you can probably swim in college, and your boyfriend will cheer for you at all your meets."

*   *   *

I RUN IT OVER IN my mind. Meeting Will, watching him make food for me, laughing with him, seeing those eyes turn from gray to blue, then back to gray. I review it the way I'd watch a race tape: the start, the first turn, the problems.

How do I adjust? I push my plate away and pick up my phone.

*   *   *

THE NEXT DAY, I EAT my Pop-Tarts in the car as we drive.

"Those names I emailed you last night, will you call them?"

"Basil, are you sure about this? The last go-around made you miserable. Mom and I were talking. We think it's time for all of us to rethink your strategy. What about getting a college scholarship instead of—"

"Dad, will you please just call the names? Set something up. I'm working on the rest."

I'm at the snack bar when Will arrives at 4:39.

"I owe you an apology."

"Okay."

He sets down a bag with two baguettes sticking out of it and unlocks the door.

"I'm sorry. For the other day."

"What the hell, Basil? I spent my own money on all that food. I came in at 4:00 a.m. to caramelize bananas for you. You *asked* me for bananas."

"It was the peanut butter."

"You said you could eat it every day!"

"I said 'every night.'"

"Is this one of your superstitions? Or am I supposed to know that Michael Phelps never eats peanut butter?"

I wince at the reference. "No. It's a me thing. I can't eat peanut butter before I swim. It sticks in my throat and slows me down. I only eat it at night."

He flips the light on and puts his bag on the counter. Koji stalks out from the locker room: 4:43.

"Yeah, well, you could have found a better way to communicate than spitting it out. On camera, no less."

"Jay Scott was staring at me; the cameras were in my face. I messed up. I was nervous, and then when you said the ingredients, I freaked out."

"That was about us—me. Those were my arepas you spat out, not a box of Pop-Tarts."

"That's what makes you different."

"Different?"

"I used to think that swimming was about endurance, and focus, and repeating tedious steps over and over and that no one who didn't swim understood that. But you show up as early as I do every day, to make your *mise en place*. It's chopping onions and other prep work, so it's probably tedious also. But to be good, you have to do it. I've watched you. You barely move when you put a dish together. You take the time to put everything where you need it. You know your kitchen as well as I know the pool. You work through injuries. This job isn't just flipping burgers for you, it's creating experiences for people—like the arepas."

We stare at each other. It's 4:45. But I can tell he's softening. I do what I would do in a race. I press harder.

"You said that cooking is all about the diner. When you cook, you want to make what I want to eat. You make me feel like you want me to like it—to like you. I want that."

"What about Koji? He told me to stay away from you."

4:46.

"Forget Koji."

"He'll be in my face in two minutes telling me to go back to the grill."

"Submergd cancelled my contract. I may not have him as a coach for much longer anyway."

"Is it that serious?"

"That and the fact that I'm losing races along with my appetite."

"I'll think about it."

It's 4:47 when I get in the pool.

My hamstring aches.

"Late," remarks Koji, "so start with back."

WILL

"WILL, BRO, YOU THINK MAYBE it's not about the food?"

Even though I know what Toby means—and that it's true—I ask him. "What, then?"

"First, it was, 'what's with this a-hole.' Then, you're all, 'he only likes hot dogs,' when that's what you're supposed to be making at a snack bar. Last week, 'waaaah, he puked up my corn thingies on national TV.' Now you're whining, 'he's sorry and he's going to lose his gold medal but he likes my food.'"

"I don't talk like that, all squeaky, but go on."

"So it's not about the food, dummy. You like him or you wouldn't be calling me about him every two seconds."

"No, it's not like that. I'm supposed to make up dishes and put out a menu. The diner decides."

"Whatever it's 'like,' you need to talk to him—*about* stuff, not just 'when do you eat peanut butter?'"

"How am I supposed to talk to him when he's either in the pool or hiding behind his coach? And I don't talk that way."

"What are *you* hiding behind, dude? If you can't find your heat, get out of the kitchen."

*   *   *

So I TRY *MISE EN place*, only I take it to another level, thinking I can free up some extra time to talk to Basil. The next morning, instead of leaving the door open, which causes trouble for him with Koji, I close the snack bar door and set up quietly. At 8:15, I raise the metal screen, ready to go. The special is up, bacon and sausages are prepped, the grill is hot.

Basil shows up, his face registering concern. "I didn't think you were here. Your door was closed."

I smile, thinking he missed me, and hand him three plates and a large cup. "I made you breakfast. Everything you like, no morning peanut butter. Pull up a stool?"

He blushes and looks down at the food. His lips are purple; the lower one juts out. When he turns to get a stool, the muscles in his neck bulge, and I get a whiff of chlorine mixed with sweat. It smells better than melting butter.

"Buckwheat pancakes with a berry coulis and creme fraiche. Don't tell Raheem it's not just a short stack with syrup."

He nods, still staring at the food, and picks up a fork.

"Scrambled eggs, French style, with chives. Bacon and home fries. Sourdough toast, with Danish butter called *Lurpak*. Guess what kind of jam it is, and you win the grand prize."

"Wow. All this and a milkshake too?"

"Banana smoothie."

He looks up at me, his big brown eyes wide. He tastes everything on the plate, then the smoothie. He leans back in his chair and, his face soft, looks at me again and says something that sounds like "ay fogatone cuz mo."

My mouth asks, "Huh?" but in response to his tone and his smile, my mind yells *Sweet!* Then, *Oh, god, maybe I do talk "that way."*

Before I get an answer, Koji interrupts us. "Basil, I didn't let you go. You owe me a kick set before you eat all that." Basil mouths *sorry*, but goes right back to the pool.

So much for *mise en place* to the next level.

*   *   *

LUNCH IS NO BETTER. Koji lets Basil order, which he does with a shaky voice. His eyes dart to Koji standing next to him; Koji's trademark frown is cutting his face in half.

I mouth "later?" to Basil, but Koji pulls him to a table before he can respond. "We need to go over your afternoon workout before I leave. I have that appointment at four."

That's my opening.

*   *   *

AT 4:30 P.M., I PULL down the metal screen. I'm a little early, but Raheem isn't around and the afternoon swimmers all went home. Toby's right. It's time to get out of the kitchen.

The pool is empty except for Basil. I take off my clogs, roll up my pants, and sit at the shallow end, dangling my legs in the water next to his lane. He notices right away, holds a single finger out of the water, and keeps going.

Okay, I can wait.

One lap later, he stops. "You're here." he says, pulling his goggles down and dipping his head to clear his ears. "You never come to the pool. Is it that late?"

"Am I interrupting?" I hope so—this was my plan.

"It's okay. Like I said before, I'm about to lose Koji. If I don't find another sponsor soon, another swimmer will hire him."

"Do you need to keep practicing?"

"At this?" He looks around the empty pool as if he's not sure where he is. "Yes, but I can take a break." He starts for the ladder.

"Wait." I stand and take off my apron and jacket. He raises his eyebrows. I kick off my pants. His mouth makes a little O when I slide into the pool next to him wearing only black boxer briefs. "Show me something."

"What?"

"I don't know. I can dog paddle, but I never took lessons."

"Never? But Toby—"

"—is the family athlete. I'm not about to compete with my jock brother."

His mouth eases into a little smile then broadens into a grin. "Stand in front of me, sideways."

When I do, he puts his left hand on my chest and his right on my lower back. I shift, surprised that his hands are warm, warmer than the water. He flinches when I let my hip brush against his swimsuit. He catches me smiling but pretends not to.

"Flex your knees and lean back."

It makes me nervous. I don't know what he plans to do and I don't like leaning backward into the water. I bend my knees, but my back is rigid.

"Relax. I've got you. Lift your feet." He moves his other hand under my back, and I flail a bit, like the blond girl in King Kong's palm.

I want to pinch my nose to keep the water out, but what am I, five? Then I remember how he let me feed him even after the peanut butter mistake, so I take a deep breath, shut my eyes, and lean back. Basil's hands hold me up; I'm floating, and they're barely touching me.

"You can open your eyes now." He stands over me, looking into my eyes and holding back a laugh.

"What's so funny?"

"Your face. You look like you think I'm going to dunk you and jump out."

Wait a minute! I meet him on his own ground—well, water—and he laughs at me? "I'm done." I find my footing and face him. My back feels cold where his hands were.

"Was it tomato?" he asks.

"What do you mean?"

"The jam with the toast this morning."

"Tomato and orange marmalade, that's right."

"You said there was a grand prize."

"What would you like?"

"'Show *me* something,'" he mimics.

We both laugh—tension dissolved—and he steps closer to me.

This is it. I put my face to his. I'm shorter, so I reach up and pull his head down. He resists. "'Relax. I've got you,'" I mimic back. "Here's your *something*."

I kiss him and taste chlorine on our lips. I slide my hand from the back of his head to his neck, surprised that his hair feels so soft. My fingers spread out against the slickness of his skin. Our bodies align; my back is against the edge of the pool. With our mouths together, I flick my tongue against his closed lips. He stiffens and pulls his face back.

"I'm not going to dunk you and jump out," I whisper, my voice husky. He leans against me; his body is smooth but unyielding, almost like flexible marble, only warm, so warm. This time he kisses me.

We're both shivering by the time we leave the water. He tosses me a towel.

"Basil, what you said earlier, while you were eating breakfast? Was it Greek?"

"Yeah. I said, '*efaga ton kosmo na se vro.*'" He repeats it slowly, twice. It sounds dark and rich, like strong coffee. "My Pappou used to say it to my Yaya. It means, 'I ate the whole world to find you.'"

BASIL

IT'S TWO WEEKS LATER. I don't have to be at the pool for team warm-ups until 7:00 a.m., but I'm here at 5:30. I'm in the water doing an easy warm-up when Koji shows up. The light is on in Will's kitchen. I didn't stop to talk. I'm completely focused.

Koji doesn't run through the race with me as he usually does. Jay Scott swims at today's meet, wearing a Submergd warm-up jacket. He's the one Koji went to watch. When I worked up the nerve to ask how it went, all Koji would say is, "He's going to be hard to beat. That guy is so intense he noticed when they used a new brand of chlorine in his pool."

Today's my last chance. I need to get it right.

I eat a banana and two hard-boiled eggs. I find a white towel in the locker room.

The other teams are gathering. The camera crew is setting up near the snack bar. It's go time.

"Hey, Ms. Alvarez?"

"Basil, good luck out there today. We're getting some shots of all the swimmers. Don't worry, we won't focus on you until later. Did you get the new warm-ups I sent?" She knows about the Submergd incident. My dad told her when he called about getting a Heat endorsement. We figured it was better to be honest. Today, Heat is testing me out.

"Right here," I hold up the jacket. "There are some important people I need you to meet. You're going to want to film this."

She humors me, pulling the cameraman over to where they set up lights and brush me with make-up. I pull on my new jacket, which has an orange wave emblazoned on the chest. Koji stands on the other side of the pool near Jay, with his arms crossed over his chest.

The snack bar window is open now, and I introduce Will.

"The Upper Collingford Swim Club has been very supportive," I tell her. "I thought I was trading lifeguarding hours for practice time and a few burgers and omelets every day. Then I found out that not only is Will a gourmet chef, but he's willing to practice on me." I'm awkward, but Ms. Alvarez seems interested, and the camera is still running.

"Basil, tell us how you do it all. You beat your own best time last week in the Individual Medley, setting a new national record. You're headed to the Olympic trials. That's a lot to accomplish at the age of sixteen."

"Honestly, this summer has been a roller coaster for me. I had some injuries and hit a rough patch. My times started getting better when two things happened. The first was that I switched gear. When you measure wins in hundredths of a second, every advantage counts. I broke my IM record the first time I wore a Heat suit."

Ms. Alvarez grins. This is my shot.

"And, second, I was lucky enough to find Will power."

"You must need a lot of willpower to train at your level."

"No, I mean I found *Will.* It sounds cheesy, but his cooking and his focus help power me through each practice and each race."

Will turns bright red. He didn't know I was going to say that. Nonetheless, he hands me the plate the way we practiced. I'm nervous as hell, but it's going okay. Even if I blow it with Heat, the look on Will's face tells me I'm winning.

I hold the plate in front of my chest and tell the story of Pappou and my early swim lessons.

The camera catches a close-up of two rectangular pockets of Will's golden, crisp, buttery pastry, stuffed with homemade strawberry jam. They're topped with honey-sweetened frosting and dusted with chia seeds instead of sugar sprinkles, for extra protein. Will and I tell the story of how we came up with the recipe for Pappou Tarts together.

Then I eat them both.

"I make him two every day, no more, no less." Something on the grill behind him is smoking, but he doesn't turn away from the camera.

"Does he have a lot of superstitions?" Ms. Alvarez asks.

Will laughs. "You have no idea. But Basil will kill me if I tell you. He says, 'you can't give the competition any advantage.'"

"It's like a secret recipe," I agree. "You keep it in your head, not on paper."

I tell Ms. Alvarez about my morning routine, my two-a-day practices, my work as a lifeguard. But I keep to myself rides home with Will, when our fingers intertwine between the seats and his car lingers in my driveway for a long time before I get out. And I don't tell her about evenings in the pool, just the two of us, and the tang of chlorine, the sound of laughter and splashing, the touch of hands on water-slick backs, arms, hips. I don't explain that after we climb out of the pool, soggy and exhausted, Will makes us dinner to eat by citronella candlelight. We evaluate new recipes and test new ways to sit as close to each other as possible, and he rewards me with another kiss for every ingredient I guess right.

Instead, I motion Koji over.

"I've been working with Basil for the past three years," Koji says. "Top-level swimmers need to learn discipline and adjustment. You discipline yourself to put in the practice time, to know the strokes, to drill the technique. When something unexpected happens, you have to figure out how to adjust for it. Basil has always had the discipline. But meeting Will was unexpected. I didn't think he would be able to fit a boyfriend into his schedule. In fact, I'm still not sure he can."

A small flame leaps up behind Will. He's completely focused on me as I interrupt.

"Koji has taught me that I constantly need to adjust to the race. If I lose my goggles in the start, I know the pool well enough to keep going. If another racer is gaining on me in the finish, I modify my stroke to meet that. Will—"

"I'm as disciplined at cooking as Basil is at swimming. We didn't have to explain that to each other. But *he* had to adjust, learn to understand my language."

"Pool talk meets kitchen chat?" She laughs. Will and I do too.

"I still want to win. But now I understand how big a part of that Will can be. Koji never lets me rest on yesterday's accomplishments anyway."

"Koji never lets Basil rest at all!"

"I have to prove myself every day—"

"—but not to me—"

"—and that's a big change—"

"—for both of us!"

Only then does Will turn to his grill. He swears as he grabs a pair of tongs and throws something in the sink. Ms. Alvarez laughs and instructs the camera to cut. They can't use the swearing part. Maybe Will did that on purpose so he wouldn't be caught burning something on film, but now is not the time to ask.

Ms. Alvarez promises to send a contract tonight for my parents to sign. She has a whole box of Heat gear for me. *Sports Illustrated* wants a photoshoot next month.

I stride to the locker room to run my playlist. I'm going to listen to Free Boyz, shave, and run through the race in my mind: the start, each split, the finish. I'm going to warm up, right side first. Then I'm going to kick Jay Scott's ass. After the race, I'll talk to Koji about tomorrow's practice and ice my hamstring.

Only then will I go find Will and ask what he ruined on the grill this morning. He'll ask me to guess what's in the pasta sauce. We'll finally have a chance to talk and to sit together, feet tangled under the table, while we share a meal. He promised strawberry milkshakes for dessert.

ABOUT TOM WILINSKY AND JEN STERNICK: Tom Wilinsky and Jen Sternick's debut novel, *Snowsisters* (Duet Books, 2018) was a Foreword INDIES finalist and won a Feathered Quill Silver Medal, the NYC Big Book Award, third place in the UK Wishing Shelf Awards and the Golden Crown Literary Society Award for YA fiction. Tom lives in New York with his partner and their beloved orange cat, Newky. He likes cold weather, old horror movies and 20th century cars. Jen lives in Rhode Island with her family and a cranky seven-toed cat named Sassy. She likes live theater, visiting any place she's never been before, and admits to a mild Twitter addiction. Find them at www.neverhaveieverbooks.com.

THE AUGUST SANDS

by Jude Sierra

CHAPTER ONE

Tommy'd been stuck in the back of the minivan for the two and a half agonizing hours it took to get from his suburban Metro Detroit home to Caseville, Michigan, during which he'd been forced to endure what seemed like his fifty-sixth viewing of *Moana*. He'd have listened to music, but his phone was an outdated model with a battery that drained way too fast. And besides, Hannah liked to keep up a constant commentary on her movie. Plus, his parents expected him to keep her occupied.

Mary Engle, otherwise known to them as Mare, was half-hidden by her garden when they finally, finally pulled up to their lakeside rental. She gave a half wave but otherwise didn't move. After seven years renting one of her cottages to them, she knew them well enough to let them do their own thing when they arrived.

Tommy clambered out of the car after Hanna and Ethan; he tripped over, then grabbed their little backpacks. Mary always let them park next to the house on the side lawn; sand and crabgrass shifted under his feet. Hannah and Ethan were running around the backyard and laughing.

"Tommy, Tommy, Tommy can we go down, will you take us down, please?"

"Please, please," Ethan tugged on Tommy's shorts.

"You guys need swimsuits," Tommy said. Past the raised deck and down a little hill, the sand was a pristine, sugar-cookie tan and the water glinted sapphire blue in the sun. Hannah and Chase hopped around, cheering madly. Tommy laughed. "Mom," he pitched his voice over the wash of water; the waves were small but the sound carried up the hill, "can I take them?"

"What?" She picked her way over to him. He relieved her of the heavy tote she was carrying over her shoulder.

"The kids want to go down. Do you want me to help unpack or take them?"

"Oh, my god, take them please." The wind tossed her hair; sun caught her new highlights and brightened her blue eyes. "Get them out of our hair while we unpack. The bathing suit bag is on the porch."

"Sweet." Tommy paused. "Wait. Is mine in there?"

"Tommy, honey, you're eighteen. You're in charge of your own packing."

Damn. He definitely packed suits, but they were buried in his suitcase.

"All right, turkeys." He put a hand on each kid's head. "Let's get ready, and I'll take you down. First one ready for sunscreen wins."

"Wins what?" Ethan looked up; suspicion was clear on his little features. Tommy might have a history of incentivizing with no actual prize in mind.

"Uh…" Tommy looked at his mom. "An extra cookie."

The look she shot him was perhaps two steps below murderous.

"It's vacation, Mom," Tommy said. "Sugar them up all day and maybe they'll crash at night."

"Thanks for the sound parenting advice." She rolled her eyes. Hannah and Ethan took off, slamming the screen door behind them.

"Ethan, man," Tommy climbed the stairs behind them, "change in the bathroom, no one needs to see your naked butt out here." He rooted in the bag for Ethan's bathing suit. "You can't just go streaking here, people are gonna be in the cottage next door at some point."

Ethan stuck his tongue out but caught the bathing suit easily.

Jerry, his stepfather, struggled up the stairs with Tommy's suitcase. "What on earth did you pack? We're only here for a week."

Tommy took the suitcase without comment. He was a problem packer, always packing alternate clothes in case he wasn't in the mood for what he chose, as well as alternate-alternate clothes in case the weather report was completely wrong. Which, come on. Michigan. The weather report was never right.

He always stayed in the smallest solo room. It was closest to the water, which meant he could hear the waves at night and watch the sunset from his bed while reading. Contradicting all advice he'd given his brother, Tommy slipped out of his clothes and into his suit without bothering to lower the blinds. The cottage next door was quiet. Its occupants must not have arrived yet. Some cottages rented to the same families year after year. Mare and her husband owned a cluster of them in varying sizes along their stretch of beachfront, but the cottage next door only had two rooms, one of which was a loft with no walls. It didn't appeal to most families.

Tommy emerged to find his mother sunscreening Ethan for him.

"I've already done Hannah," his mom said. "Get yours done and you're good to go."

Tommy resisted, barely, rolling his eyes. He was too old to be mothered. A month from now he'd be at college, in charge of himself. At eighteen, Tommy was considerably older than his siblings, Hannah and Ethan, who were nine and six. Tommy had helped take care of them from the beginning, had often felt a complicated twist of resentment and fondness for them. They were Jerry's kids from his previous marriage, but they'd been four and one when Jerry married Tommy's mom. Soon, he'd be gone. He wasn't sure who would miss whom more, the kids or himself.

The night he'd gotten his acceptance letter to Michigan State, he'd gone to bed buzzing with excitement. It took him less than half an hour to realize he had no idea how to picture himself in a new life, without his siblings, his parents, his home. These were signposts for who he was, how he defined himself: the brother, the helpful son, the good kid who always made the right choices because he was so scared of the consequences that came with making mistakes. Everyone said college was a time for making mistakes. Tommy wanted to be the kid who could let go, have slightly reckless fun, but he couldn't really picture a version of himself that was okay with not knowing what might come next.

Vibrating with impatience, the kids ran onto the grass, while he slathered himself up, then dashed down the stairs. "Not the water," he called. "I need to check for rip currents!" He could have saved his breath; they were both already digging through Mary's tub of beach toys. The wind wasn't up, and he didn't think there'd been a storm lately, but the sandbar could be deceptive. Last year they'd let Hannah go out to it, and it turned out it wasn't where it seemed to be, where it had been for the last two days.

Tommy winced and hopped over a shallow wave. The cold water was unexpected on such a warm day, and he had to resist the urge to cover his nuts. On the sandbar, the water was knee-deep and warm. The sky was cerulean all around, unbroken by clouds. To the southwest, the shoreline curved until it was almost directly west, where they watched the sun set every night.

The kids were busily digging at the shoreline, filling buckets with the wet, heavy sand. Tommy waded toward them, letting his body acclimate to the water until it had gone from fucking freezing to merely bracing. He took it all in. Tommy loved it here and he loved having his family here. August was his favorite time of year. Along the south slope of the hill leading to the cottage, the landscape was natural. Mare's cottage sat along the stretch of public beach. Queen Anne's lace, ditch lilies, and chicory bloomed among the tall grasses.

Tommy was pulled from his reverie by the slam of a car door and a spill of laughter carrying over the water. Two men came around to let themselves into the tiny cottage next to his family's. It was impossible to judge the men's ages from his location, but they seemed to be on the younger side. After them, a girl with a backpack and suitcase came around the corner. Her short shorts and a tank top were a clear giveaway: probably college-age. Boisterous laughter carried on the wind. For a moment, jealousy washed through Tommy. He was on the verge of leaving home, but, rather than spending time with his friends, he was stuck with his family for a whole week. His best friend Sean was hosting a bonfire and cookout as a final goodbye this weekend, and Tommy was missing it. He'd been reduced to babysitter for a week.

Being a teenager sucked sometimes. A lot. Mostly.

"Tommy, Tommy, can I come in?" Hannah was at the water's edge.

"Sure," he said, laughing as she pranced into the water. A wave hit her square in the face, and she shrieked with laughter. Tommy waded toward her, scooped her up, and dropped her back in.

"Again! Do it again!"

He horsed around in the water with her until they were both exhausted. He towed her back in when her little lips took on a blue tinge. The sun began its slide toward the horizon, and a little wind picked up.

By the time he had Hannah burritoed in a towel, their mom was calling them. Ethan was covered head to toe in sand despite not having gone in the water at all. Tommy worked on brushing and shaking it off. There was nothing more annoying than sand tracked into the cottage.

"I'll take it from here," Jerry said. "Come on, Ethan, let's play on the porch until Hannah's out of the shower."

Tommy wrapped up in an extra towel his mother had put out and parked himself on the porch as well. Mare's cottage had a big, screened-in porch where they sat at night playing games, where they set up a towel rack to dry towels and bathing suits, and where they often threw picnic lunches.

Maybe it wasn't a bonfire with his friends, but Tommy loved the familiarity of vacation rituals and, although he'd never admit it, the focused time with his family and his siblings. Tonight they'd eat dinner out here and watch the sunset paint the sky purple and pink and gild the black water; they'd eat too many Skittles and M&M's and play cards until they ached with laughter.

Maybe being stuck with his family wasn't such a bad thing, after all.

CHAPTER TWO

BY NOON THE NEXT DAY, it seemed like the Worst Day Ever. Tommy'd rarely seen Hannah be such a brat. He had no idea what the cause was—lack of sleep maybe—but he didn't much care by the fourth time he had to break up a fight between her and Ethan. He also really cared that his mother was complacently reading a book and, you know, not *mothering*.

Tommy was smart enough not to say that out loud but he thought it pretty hard in her direction when he went back to his lounge chair.

"Tommy, honey, take a breath," Elise said, turning a page. "You have to tune them out. Let them work it out. So long is no one is hurt or in danger, a little screeching won't kill anyone."

"Mom." Tommy took a deep breath and then another, and they were both utterly useless in calming him. "I *can't* tune them out. They're at volume nine."

"Oh, I'd only give them a seven out of ten," she said. "You look warm, honey. Why don't you go for a walk? The air is cooler by the edge of the water."

"You sure?"

"Tommy, I didn't bring you on vacation to babysit your siblings the whole time." Her sunglasses covered about half her face, but he'd bet money that she was rolling her eyes at him.

"Okay." Tommy ran up to the cottage to grab his phone and earbuds. He pulled on a shirt, slipped his phone into a pocket, and headed toward the public park farther down the eastern shoreline.

Tommy waded, enjoying the suck and pull of sand as each small wave rushed over his feet. The sand was clear of debris and soft and there no clumps of seaweed to avoid. Often, after a storm came through, they'd find the waterline strewn with seaweed and washes of little shells swathed over large portions of beach. Hannah and Ethan would have a field day picking buckets of them, which his mom would secretly throw away before they could beg to take them all home to make a "collection."

Twenty One Pilots pulsed through his earbuds loudly enough to drown out the cry of the gulls, the chatter of the beachgoers he walked past, and even the ever-present susurration of the water. Right at the horizon, he could see the steady progress of a lake freighter. He was watching it when he got hit square in the chest by a football.

"*Fuck*." Tommy ripped out his ear buds. *Ow*, that hurt.

"Oh, man, I am so sorry." It was one of the guys he'd seen last night from the cottage next door. And he was *cute*: all dark hair and easy smile, long-limbed but stockier than Tommy. "I tried to call out, but—"

"Yeah, my music was pretty loud," Tommy said. He tried to drape his earbuds around his neck casually, hoping the movement might invite further interaction. He fumbled with them and ended up draping the tangled mess over his right shoulder. The guy watched with amused interest and didn't say anything. Tommy looked down and noted that the football was at his feet. *Oh*.

"Oh, uh, sorry about that," he said. His earphones fell into the sand when he bent over to pick up the football.

"No worries." The guy was kind enough not to laugh, but amusement was evident in the crinkled corners of his eyes. He held out a hand. "I'm Chase."

Tommy had begun to extend the football when he realized Chase was actually going for a handshake. This time he did close his eyes in embarrassment.

"I'm Tommy," he said. Chase's palm was smooth and warm. His messy, dark hair was caught in the breeze, which was picking up off the water. "I'm sorry." He managed to actually hold out the football.

"Stop apologizing, really. It's okay. I'm the one who assaulted you with sporting goods," Chase said. One of his friends called out from farther down the beach; with enviable grace and coordination he tossed the ball to him. Tommy expected him to walk away, but he didn't. He turned back toward him and pushed up his sunglasses. His eyes were a strange hazel, almost olive green. Maybe they'd change in the light. Tommy thought, wildly, of getting to observe them in different lights and then squashed the notion. Belatedly he realized it was his turn to speak.

"So…"

"You here for the week?" Chase asked casually, as if Tommy weren't the worst at conversation with a stranger, ever.

"Yeah, I come with my family every year."

"Those your siblings, last night?"

"Oh, yeah." Tommy was surprised he'd been noticed. "Hannah and Ethan."

"That's cool. I always wanted siblings."

"Ooh, an only child," Tommy said. "I've always wanted to know how the other half lives."

Chase's smile was bright and quick. He probably never had to worry about first impressions, not with a face like that. "Wanna come meet my cousins? We're neighbors for a week, right?"

Tommy bit down on the inside of his check, trying not to betray an uncool level of excitement. "Sure, that would be awesome."

Chase gestured with his shoulder, and Tommy followed. He tried it ignore the heat in his belly whenever Chase's shoulder brushed his. He walked the water's edge, splashing and wishing he had sunglasses too. It was so much easier to check someone out from behind a screen that shielded the play of thoughts people always told him were much too easy to read.

Chase's cousin threw the ball. Chase caught it easily, jostling Tommy in the process. His laughter was easy and infectious.

"Hey, guys, this is Tommy. I found him wandering the shore alone," Chase said.

"Hey." The other guy extended a sandy hand. "I'm Jake." He pointed up toward the grass, where a girl was laying out towels to dry. "That's my sister, Cheryl."

Tommy waved and told himself this was easy. That it could be easy. That it should be easy. He'd have to master this soon enough, meeting new people at college. Tommy grew up with the same friends his entire life. He'd gone to the same tiny Catholic school with the same students since he was a little kid. His awkwardness in new situations was rarely a problem when everyone already knew him. And okay, it sucked sometimes (a lot), being a prepackaged version of Tommy who fit into a neat box made of other people's perceptions and expectations. That's how high school was, right? Everyone fit into their own slot, and the lives they made after high school were the ones that mattered. People became who they wanted to be, if it all went okay.

Tommy was messy and uncoordinated, unsure of each movement, worrying each word like a stone in his mouth. And yeah, he often despaired over his inability to enter new situations without being horrendously awkward, sure it would never go away. The sun kissed Chase's skin, which was shining and slick with sweat and sunscreen. Tommy knew it wasn't fair to assume that a guy who looked like that, who moved with ease and confidence, never felt as awkward and wrong as he did, but he was going to do it anyway.

"I have to warn you, I have the literally worst hand-eye coordination." Tommy forced himself to smile, to banter, knowing that if he had long enough to warm up, the smile would be genuine. He just had to fake being himself until…he could be himself.

"Well, that always spices up a game of catch," Chase said. He lobbed the ball at Tommy without warning, and Tommy caught it more out of instinct than skill. He passed it back to Jake before playfully kicking some sand at Chase.

An hour later they were all sweat-soaked and sandy and, when Cheryl came with hot dogs, unanimously starving. "Mom sent me down with sustenance."

"Oh." That was his cue. "I'll let you guys eat in peace."

"No, man, stay." Jake, focused on the potato chip bag he was trying to open, shot him a smile.

"We have plenty," Cheryl said. "Really."

The warmth of welcome washed through him. "Thanks."

"Ok, wait. No ketchup? Mustard?" Chase frowned.

"My hands were full. Take your complaint somewhere else. Or up to the grill station Mom has going; they have stuff." Chase ran up to their cottage to get condiments and drinks. Tommy accepted a paper plate and hesitated. *You've been invited.* He took a hot dog gingerly.

"Relish too!" Tommy met Chase's eyes as he bounded down the stairs. Heat flashed through him, between them. Not that he'd ever had someone to flirt with, but Tommy was relatively sure that there was something sparking, something flirtier than normal in that look.

"You're here with family? Chase said you all are cousins."

"Mmhmm." Cheryl nodded toward the deck to their left. It was larger than the one that came with Tommy's cottage. "It's our parents' twentieth wedding anniversary, so a bunch of family thought they'd have a celebratory week."

"You'd think they might want a solo vacation," Tommy said. Then, "Oh, shit, was that rude?"

"Not at all," Cheryl said, drowning her hot dog in ketchup.

"Our parents are close friends," Chase said. "So they invited us. And then Aunt Katie found out and…it grew."

"It's nice though. Like a big family reunion. Plus, we have each other and can do our own thing." Jake crammed half a hot dog into his mouth. "They even let us share our own cottage, away from the adults and the little kids too. It's the tiny one, right behind yours?"

"Wow, that's awesome." Tommy took a handful of chips, mindful of talking with his mouth full. "We've always just come the five of us."

"So basically, it's just your family?" Cheryl asked.

"Yup. I get a lot of reading done. And you know, my siblings can be fun. Not that it's the same as having, you know," he paused, wondering how to word it without sounding like he was inviting himself to hang out with them, "people my age around. I mean. Like family, and—"

"Well, then this is your lucky year," Chase bumped shoulders with him. "Because this year, you have us."

Tommy flushed and looked down; ketchup from his hotdog had plopped onto his lap. He felt better then, less as if he'd been invited out of politeness. It made laughing over Cheryl's burnt hot dogs easier. It made observing their banter, even jumping in a time or two, easier.

"You like Coke?" Chase asked after a bit, smoothing over the silence. Tommy's smile was permission enough for Chase to crack one open one-handed.

By the time Tommy checked his phone, he was surprised to see hours had passed. The agitation and irritation inspired by his siblings was long forgotten; even more, he was relieved at having passed a small test, at finding that he could challenge himself to come out of his shell.

"Crap, I gotta go," he said, not bothering to hide his regret. "Got family stuff tonight."

"That's cool," Jake said. "We'll see you later."

"You're here for the week though, right?" Chase asked. Tommy bit his lip and turned his face away to hide a wide smile.

"Yes."

"Sweet." Chase stood up and brushed sand from his shorts. Tommy fell in step with him automatically, realizing belatedly that Chase was walking him home. It was cute, considering that their cottages were a stone's throw from each other. "You able to hang out again?"

"Definitely," Tommy said. Alone, he felt better letting himself smile. Chase's directness was refreshing; Tommy didn't have to guess at his interest now, because the darted looks from Tommy's eyes to his lips and the slow heat of his smile said it all.

"Have a good night then," Chase turned away with a final glance over his shoulder. Tommy could see Cheryl stretching out on a chaise lounge in the sand. Her laughter was a tease directed toward Chase, who shook his head. His words were caught by the wind. Tommy forced himself to go in, lest he get caught staring, but he was smiling so hard his cheeks hurt.

CHAPTER THREE

ON MONDAY, EVERYTHING AND NOTHING in Tommy's life changed.

He played with Hannah and Ethan. He helped get them get lunch and slayed both his mom and dad during their evening round of Push. He spent so much time out on the beach that he went to bed that night with an uncharacteristic sunburn.

At the same time, though, there was Chase. They didn't spend the whole day with each other, exactly. But they sure spent a lot of it together. And when they weren't together, Tommy couldn't help but track Chase's movements along the beach. Jerry had had an outright laugh at him at one point; Tommy had been watching Chase as he took his turn with a paddleboard his aunt had rented.

"You have it so bad, buddy," Jerry had said.

"Shut up," Tommy'd said, shoulders up by his ears, but he'd laughed too. Chase fell off the board but surfaced laughing; water was slick and streaming down his chest. Tommy did have it bad. That didn't stop him from watching all Chase's abysmal attempts at paddle boarding or staring as he made his way out of the water and up to the cottages for lunch.

Tommy ate his own lunch with Ethan and Hannah, then playing the world's most repetitive game of I Spy, before escaping to the beach without even asking his mom to watch the kids. They were her kids, after all. Right? *Ugh*. Tommy squashed guilt and reminded himself it was his vacation too. He was allowed to drowse on the beach with a book.

"Hey, wanna go for a walk?" Chase caught Tommy off guard; he had fallen asleep only about twenty pages into his book. Tommy's family must have come down at some point because Jerry was playing catch with Hannah and Ethan while his mother relaxed on a lounge chair next to him.

"Yeah!" Tommy sat up in a flurry of sand. "I mean," he cleared his throat. "Yes, that would be cool."

"Have fun, kids," Elise said, unabashedly amused. Tommy's withering glare was completely lost behind his sunglasses, and, while Chase didn't appear to be laughing at him, he was clearly definitely amused. Tommy brushed sand from his arms and legs with as much dignity as he could muster.

"Hold on a sec," Tommy said, leaving Chase to make small talk with his mom—*please, god, let her be subtle*—while he ran up to the cottage to grab a tank top and two small bottles of water. He was back seconds later, out of breath and juggling the bottles and the tank top, which he had somehow not thought to put on upstairs. Chase was telling his mom a story about his parents; he had her laughing, and Tommy spared a second to be thankful she wasn't doing the talking. "Here. Uh—" He tried to hand Chase a bottle of water but almost dropped both.

"I can take them," Chase said, nodding at the tank top, "so you can get that on."

Tommy looked down, overcome by an unbidden but undeniably compelling image of Chase telling him to take it off, or taking it off himself.

"Have fun, kiddo," Tommy's mom said, poking him in the thigh with her toes. "Dinner's at five thirty, okay?"

"Yeah, sure," Tommy said. He didn't want to assume Chase wanted to spend the next four hours with him; he aimed for dismissive or casual but probably missed the mark. Tommy had very little chill on a good day, much less in the vicinity of a cute boy shining with sunscreen and sweat and beaming welcoming smiles at him. His attempt at chill was nothing more than breathless and higher pitched than usual. "So," he turned to Chase, trying harder to modulate his voice. "Which way?"

Chase gestured toward the west. He high-fived Ethan, who was digging himself a "pool" at the edge of the water.

The long stretch of beach curving ahead of them was empty. They walked at the waterline so the water rushed over their feet, swallowing their footprints.

"Do you all live near each other?"

"No. We all live in Michigan. But my Aunt Sharon and Uncle Nick live up in Cheboygan. My other aunt lives in Gaylord."

"A northern family, I see. And you guys?"

"Grand Rapids," Chase said.

"You really made a trek to get here—all of you, I mean."

"You live closer, I assume?"

"We live in the metro Detroit area. Maybe like a two-and-a-half hour drive."

Chase's hand brushed against Tommy's as they walked. He resisted the urge to lean closer for more accidental touches.

"So, not exactly close by either," Chase said, looking at Tommy over the top of his sunglasses. Tommy shrugged. The sun lit all of the gold hues in Chase's eyes, giving the impression that his hazel eyes were illuminated from within.

"True. I guess I was thinking about how far from me all of you live." They stepped over an outcrop of stones and dunes, then waded to the beach beyond it. Up ahead was another public beach. "I've never been farther from home than this."

"Really?" Chase slowed, pushed up his sunglasses, and rested them in his wind-tousled his hair. It was less styled than it had been yesterday and hung over his forehead. Beautifully thick, it looked soft to the touch.

Tommy shrugged. "My parents are always running around, juggling the kids and activities and working."

"Well, what about you?"

"I'm not about to take a scenic tour of the state on my own," Tommy said. He bumped into Chase, daring and playful.

"No, I meant, aren't they busy with you too? You made it sound like…" Chase turned to keep walking. Tommy followed, waiting for the rest of his sentence. He tried to curb his impatience when it seemed that none was forthcoming.

"Like what?" he prompted finally.

"Like you're on the outside." Chase shrugged. "Never mind, I shouldn't have—that sounded judgmental, and it's not my business."

"Hey, it's okay." Tommy touched Chase's arm, fingers fleeting, just the barest memory of Chase's warm skin to tuck away. "You're not wrong." He paused to clear his throat. "I mean, it's not quite like that. I have a lot of activities, too, and I can drive. So I usually do my own thing and help them out when they need me. So, I'm not, like, neglected or anything." He rolled his eyes. Ethan and Hannah were a handful, and he did sometimes resent how much his parents depended on him. He wasn't about to spill his resentments at a stranger's feet, even if that stranger *was* crazy hot and interested.

"What do you do?"

"Oh, god, I was doing so much." Tommy ticked items off on his fingers. "Theater, school newspaper, yearbook committee, National Honor Society, which of course includes service hours."

"Holy crap, when do you sleep? Why would you do that to yourself?"

Tommy laughed, taking the teasing as it was meant. "To get into a good college. That's what my parents kept telling me. To pad my applications and all that."

"Did you?" Chase stooped to pick up a shell. The beach here was littered with tiny shells, broken and ground down by waves. This one was larger, pink in the center, and unbroken.

"I got into a few. It didn't matter in the end." Tommy kicked at the water. Foam from the waves coated his foot.

"Why not?"

"I always wanted to go to Michigan State. I applied even though my parents didn't really want me to. Told them it was my safety school."

"Why didn't they want you to go there?" They reached the near end of the public beach.

Uncomfortable with the turn in conversation, Tommy gestured toward the tree line. "Have you been to the playground with your other cousins? The younger ones, I mean."

Chase paused, as though he was trying to read Tommy's face, then shrugged, accepting the change in subject. "No, I didn't know there was one."

"Come on, I'll show you. It's a nice distraction when the little kids get stir crazy."

They picked their way through the sharp grass and over a small incline. The playground had a wooden roundabout that Tommy knew would never be allowed on newer playgrounds. Both Hannah and Ethan had fallen off of it when the momentum from spinning got too strong. Still, they always begged him to spin it for them. When their parents weren't around, he did. A few scraped knees never killed anyone.

The playground was empty. The tall trees created a hushed canopy.

"Come on," Chase caught his hand briefly, tugging him toward the swings. He let go too soon, so much sooner than Tommy would want. Reading into the touch wouldn't help the burgeoning hardcore crush. It was a friendly touch and nothing more. He followed gamely. Chase settled on a swing and nodded at the one next to him. Tommy sat, watching as Chase built momentum. Tommy listened to the quiet of the trees, searched for the sound of water, and enjoyed the pocket of calm. Chase slowed his swinging after a few minutes.

"What about you?" Tommy asked.

"What do you mean?"

"You're graduating from high school, too, right?"

"Oh! Yeah. I'm going to Tulane."

"Wow." Tommy let that sink in. "God, that's so far away,"

"Yeah," Chase said. He rested his head against the swing chain. "It'll be weird, being so far from home, but I'm really excited."

I'm terrified. Tommy swallowed the words. How embarrassing, to be so nervous about moving one hour from his family when this boy was traveling almost an entire country away.

"Sounds like you're an adventure seeker." Tommy said. The smile he got, wide and warm, was worth hiding his anxieties and insecurities. Chase's sunglasses were pushed up; his hair was a mess above them, and his were eyes bright and beautifully framed by dark lashes. Chase did seem interested in him, and no one would be interested in a boy so cowardly he was scared to leave a home he sometimes got very tired of.

Louisiana, though, that was something. Chase was something, something else. And this moment, fingertips still tingling from Chase's touch, what was that? Tommy met Chase's eyes and matched his smile. It took some work and wasn't as genuine. But then again, Chase didn't know him well enough to read him. This—this smile and the brief touch of Chase's fingers curling around his, the assessing and interested gaze—was a blip. Two lives colliding for the briefest moment. Tommy had never had this: a boy interested in him, a boy who wasn't hiding it, an opportunity.

And in the end, it would amount to nothing. It would come and go, and who would Tommy be then?

Chase stopped swinging. Tommy wasn't sure what his face was doing, but it was enough to give Chase pause. Chase closed his hand around Tommy's forearm. His touch was electrifying, too much despite being almost nothing at all. Suspended in the moment, Tommy had to catch his breath.

On the beach, a child wailed. The suddenness of the cry broke their moment.

"We should get back," Tommy said. He stood and tried so, so hard not to catalogue the ways the simplest touch had awakened his whole body. In fact, he had to push the thought away.

"Okay." Chase stood, allowing Tommy to redirect them yet again.

Tommy lingered in bed on Tuesday as long as he dared. Gray clouds scudded in low, but his weather app assured him it would be warm and mostly sunny in the afternoon. He thumbed over to his message app. Texts exchanged with Chase ran late into the night.

Chase: Epic Volleyball tourney planned today. Be on our team?

Tommy: Are you looking to epically lose? ;)

Chase: Looking for an epic good time

Tommy had given himself a good five minutes to settle the flutters in his stomach that one set off.

Tommy: Can't say no to that.

With breakfast came the rude smack of reality.

"This is a family vacation, Thomas," his mother said, plopping pancakes onto his plate. Tommy thumbed up syrup that was splattered on the tablecloth.

"I know! God, I know. I'm here, aren't I?" His shoulders, taut and pulled up, began to ache.

"Sleeping in a cottage doesn't imply active participation in a family vacation. Actually doing stuff does."

Across from him Jerry's eyes meet his, sympathetic but silent. Traitor.

"You've got to be kidding! Haven't I been watching the kids, taking them swimming, helping with lunches and sunscreen and playing freaking *ice cream palace* with buckets of sand for hours? Mom, I'm *eighteen*."

Elise set down a bowl of fresh fruit hard enough that he worried for its continued structural integrity.

"And just what does that mean?" Jeez, his mom could freeze water when she was pissed.

"That it's not always fun! That there are kids my age up here, *finally*, and it's been nice to spend a little time with them." Tommy threw his hands up. He tried to leave the table, but the heavy wooden chair caught on a deck plank, effectively ruining his snit. "Look, Mom." He took a deep breath and tried to settle his thumping heart. "I do love coming here. And I love playing with Hanna and Ethan. Trust me, I want this family time, because soon–" His voice broke, which caught her attention. Jerry put his fork down and cradled his coffee while watching with careful eyes.

"Tommy, we're still always going to do these family things," he said. "You'll always be welcome."

"What?" His mom turned to Jerry. "You say that like there would be a reason for him not to feel welcome."

"You mean, like I might choose not to come," Tommy clarified, holding Jerry's gaze. Jerry nods.

"Well, that's— That's just— Of course— " She stopped and gathered herself. Unasked, she spooned fruit onto his plate, directly into the syrup pooled to the side of his pancake. Gross. Still, he ate it, just to create space between their words and too many feelings. He wanted to reassure her, tell her of course he'd keep coming with them. Mostly, he *was* confident he wouldn't want to miss this. But everything—everything—was about to change, and he had no idea what that really meant.

"Mom." He couldn't take the silence anymore. "C'mon." He didn't clarify what he wanted, because he didn't know. But he really hated her being mad at him. He really, really, didn't feel like shopping in tiny tourist traps and eating ice cream and going to the vintage motorhome expo Jerry was so excited to see.

"You'll have a family day tomorrow." Elise compromised, voice steel and eyes tight. "We're going to the arboretum."

"Of course." An easy promise and a simple compromise. He loved the arboretum. It was by far his favorite place in Caseville.

"And you'll make smart choices." The look on her face brokered no give, no other option than agreement—which he would give anyway.

"Mom, I always make smart choices." The levity fell flat. "No, really. I've worked hard to be responsible and make good choices all my life, even when there was a lot of pressure this last year not to." Tommy didn't want to be that kid who let too loose in college, who had been so straight-laced he had no idea how to manage newfound freedom. Every choice he'd made— drinks turned down, parties he attended as the designated driver, gatherings he avoided because there would be drugs there—had been conscious and deliberate. Maybe that was partly because he was scared, but also because he was *responsible*. "I've always made those choices for *me* though. I don't make them because you force me. I'd really like it if you gave me more credit than this."

"You're right. I'm sorry." She squeezed his hand. All of the unsaid, potential words hanging in the air, heavy as rain-laden clouds, went unspoken. Tommy forced himself to finish breakfast, even if it sat like rocks in his stomach.

EVERY YEAR, HIS FAMILY SUITED up and went for a hike at the Huron County Nature Center & Wilderness Arboretum. Despite it being summer, long sleeves, pants, even hooded sweaters were necessary. The arboretum was beautiful, in spirit and place. But also swarmed with mosquitos.

The evening before, a storm unlike they'd never experienced in all the years they'd been coming had torn through, leaving them powerless. In the late afternoon, the clouds had gathered, dark and rich gray against waters that were impossibly teal. He'd instagrammed a picture. Ten minutes later the storm hit the house so hard it shook with winds so strong he'd struggled to close the inner door from the porch. Out back, between the cottage and Mare's garage, Jerry and Greg, Mare's partner, struggled to pull the flaming grill into the garage. Greg's hat was sucked up into the wind, and some of Mare's roof tiles sheered away.

As quickly as it had come, it was gone. Within an hour, the sun shone weakly, and they were trying to determine how long they would be without power. The storm had cut through the thumb of Michigan's mitten, leaving thousands without power. Brisk wind averaging twenty miles per hour had made it impossible to go near the water in the storm's wake. Jerry had tried, gamely, to make a sheltered fort area for the kids to play in. Without power, they knew it was only a matter of time before the kids were stir crazy. But no matter what they did, the wind picked up the sand, pelting them. The water was rough and too cold for swimming.

Warmer clothes worked well for their trip, and the winds were not nearly as rough inland, especially once they were under the canopy of ancient trees.

Every year, they paused at the start of the path into the trees, and Jerry let the kids choose their route. "Remember the numbers, kids, because you're gonna be the guides."

Ethan pointed to the very top of the map. "Up to station seven," he said.

"Can we go over the boardwalk?" Hannah asked. Ethan traced the path that would take them through the marsh and to the end of the trail before it naturally doubled back.

"Of course you both pick the longest trail," Tommy said. He poked Ethan's side, eliciting giggles. "You're way too old for anyone to carry you. You'll have to soldier on when you get tired."

"We won't get tired," Hannah promised. Tommy rolled his eyes at his mom, who shrugged. They would; they always did.

At first, they searched for deer and raccoons. Ethan was on a salamander kick, having just read about them. Any time a leaf so much as rustled, he insisted it must be a salamander. They all played along. Tommy pointed to birch bark, curled like white paper in the underbrush. Here, somehow, the birch trees seemed to have avoided or survived the birch borers which had killed off so many others throughout Michigan.

"We'll never spot animals if you don't shush a little," Jerry noted placidly when Ethan began to shout about a chickadee. Why he was so excited by a bird they saw daily at their own bird feeder, Tommy didn't know.

Half an hour later, Tommy lagged behind. The forest breathed green, trees teeming with something old and calm. Far above him, the trees muttered, chatting with the wind. He closed his eyes and soaked in the palpable magic. When he opened his eyes, his family were far ahead of him. His mother tossed a look over her shoulder just before they disappeared over a hill. He gestured to his left, indicating he was going to go his own way. With a half wave, she walked on. A little way down the fork in the path, he came across a small wooden structure with benches that overlooked a small hill. The forest floor was carpeted in ferns and small plants. Squirrels rustled among fallen branches. He took a few pictures and moved on, crossed the low planks over muddy ground that led to a raised boardwalk with a beautiful view of marsh and swamp grasses. Soon enough his family would meet him from the opposite direction, but, for now, he allowed himself some reflective moments. The sun was bright, but the day was still cool. The trees stirred. Years of visits had taught him to balance soaking in these vistas with helping to manage his siblings, who, year after year, insisted on trying to climb the railings to see better. Somehow, he'd never been here alone.

Many new moments were coming soon. No, Tommy would not be alone; he'd have a roommate and friends and classmates. But he might never be *this* Tommy ever again. He would always be a shadow, a new version imprinted on the collective memory of his family. Stomach dropping, Tommy let himself consider, really and truly for the first time, whether he was ready for that.

CHAPTER FOUR

BREAKFAST THURSDAY WAS DRY CEREAL and apples: fruit that hadn't spoiled. The cottage was still dark. Mare kept them updated on the constantly changing estimates for when power would come back. She'd been promised it would be sometime that day.

"If it doesn't come back on, Jerry, I think we should consider a hotel or home." Elise sighed. Hanna and Ethan were fighting over a puzzle Tommy had set down for them. The wind had died down a little, but the water was still rough.

"We can wait it out for the day. Mare said the wind should ease up by afternoon. We can go putt-putting."

"Really? I—" Tommy paused at the loud knock on the back door.

Chase huddled in the alcove between buildings. "Hey, you," he said with a tentative smile. They'd texted a time or two yesterday, but both had wanted to conserve battery power on their phones. "Still doing the family-only thing?"

Tommy stepped out and spoke quietly. "Oh, my god, I hope not, I need a break like *whoa*."

"Well, if you want, we're having a big euchre tournament. You're all welcome to come."

"All?" Tommy leaned against the wall, arms behind his back and one foot propped up behind him, daring and exposed and utterly unlike himself. The only flirting he knew how to do was borrowed from movies.

"Well, I definitely need a partner, but I know you're all probably bored. The littles are going to have their own card games."

"I'll ask. I mean, I'm a yes," he promised recklessly, not really caring if his mother was okay with it. After their fight Tuesday and the tension Wednesday, and after heavy reflection and a growing understanding of what independence may mean for him, Tommy wanted to make a choice for himself, unapologetically and selfishly.

Well, he'd probably still be a little worried that his mom would be upset, but Rome wasn't built in a day.

IN THE END, HANNAH AND Ethan voted for a trip to mini golf; Tommy was more grateful than he should have been, both for the break from his family and for the potential of more flirtation with Chase without his parents' observation.

Chase's family was loud and comfortable. Their banter was inappropriate and hilarious; Tommy hadn't laughed so hard in a long time. Unfortunately, he wasn't terrifically skilled at euchre, and he and Chase were perhaps not the best partners, especially because Chase kept knocking his feet against Tommy's under the table. It was distracting, but also more exciting than it should be. Eliminated early, Chase sat him in a corner to teach him a speed game called Oh Heck.

"Oh, my god, stop, stop, stop!" While he might have picked up on the gist of the game and the rules, he by no means was experienced enough to match Chase's speed.

"Heck!" Chase called, arms in the air when he played his last card. Tommy threw his cards at him, laughing through his protests.

"Aren't you supposed to take it easy on me? I'm new!"

"No mercy," Chase said. "Go big or go home. Accept nothing but the—"

"No more platitudes," Tommy was laughing too hard to do more than poke Chase with his foot. Across the room, Jake cheered—he and his mom were slaying all of their opponents.

"This is a nice cottage," Tommy said. He started sorting cards with Chase. "It's airy."

"Haven't you ever been in here before? You've been coming here for years."

"No, I've never seen any of the other cottages."

Chase took Tommy's deck and wordlessly put it in its box.

"We done?" Tommy cocked his head.

"Do you want to? See the others?" Chase cleared his throat. "You can see ours, if you want."

"Oh," Tommy said. This wasn't an invitation, like, *invitation* was it? "Yeah, sure. If that's fine with—"

"Oh, no one minds," Chase said easily. Tommy marveled at this and at the other hints of freedom with which he'd seen Chase's parents entrust him.

"Yeah." He could be brave. Invitation or not, Tommy thought that maybe the chance would be worth it.

Bravery, apparently, took him only so far. The cottage Chase shared with his cousins was small: a little room with a twin bed, a loft, and a pull-out couch that had been messily pushed back together so sheets and blankets trailed from between the cushions.

Chase leaned against the wood paneled wall in the "hall" outside what he'd said was his room.

"Rock, paper, scissors," he explained. "Cheryl has the loft."

"Cozy." Tommy stood, arms akimbo, unsure where he was meant to be. There was hardly room to move; almost any spot was in most rooms at once. The kitchen was nothing more than a fridge, a two-burner stove, and a counter the size of a postage stamp. His stomach and chest fizzed.

"Hey, wanna play again? I'm not sure I'm really getting it." Not at all the flirtatious gambit he'd hoped for. Cracking under pressure, he offered a stalling tactic that sounded silly even to his own ears.

Chase's smile was easy; it always seemed to be. "Sure."

Tommy's awkwardness could do nothing but melt in the comfort and camaraderie that came along with playing the card game. The wind spoke, a hollow hum that echoed through the windows, but there was also a lot of laughter. As Tommy improved, so did his competitiveness, and what started as friendly trash talk quickly devolved into slapping each other's hands through gales of laughter and tussling over cards through false accusations of cheating.

"You did that on purpose," Tommy said, breathless and still giggling.

"What?" Chase pretended to order the center cards Tommy was accusing him of scattering, "I'd never cheat."

"You just can't stand to lose to the new kid." Tommy grabbed Chase's hand before he could mess up the cards any further but stopped dead when Chase wrapped his fingers around his hand. Tommy ordered himself to inhale; he was just getting started on that when Chase kissed him.

It was over before Tommy's brain could wrap around it—
his first kiss!—but just as he was sternly ordering himself to do
something, anything, Chase leaned over again, slowly, with one
hand splayed on the scattered cards and one coming to rest on
the curve of Tommy's neck. His thumb was under Tommy's ear,
and his lips were a little chapped and much, much more confident
than Tommy's.

"Okay?" Chase asked; Tommy wasn't sure if it was a request
for permission or checking to make sure he was fine. Either way,
the only answer was *yes*, and although he couldn't bring himself
to say it, *please do it again.*

His face must have said it for him, because this time Chase
telegraphed what he was going to do next, from the flick of his
eyes over Tommy's lips to the careful hand he put on Tommy's
knee. He closed his eyes before their lips touched. Tommy
didn't, though; he wanted to be wide-eyed, to memorize every
second from the flutter of Chase's black eyelashes to the way the
light faded to gray as more clouds rolled in. Another storm was
brewing, perhaps; but it was nothing, *nothing* compared to the
rolling swell of need and nerves and hunger swallowing Tommy
in this moment.

Tommy's lips tingled, damp where Chase had very carefully
sucked at his lower lip. He pulled back, hoping to see Chase's
eyes flutter open, to read pleasure or happiness in them, to know
with a look that he wasn't failing at this one thing too. A kiss was
something so simple on paper, but an unknown with too many
potentials in action.

"Okay?" It was his turn to ask and to hope Chase understood
what he meant.

"Really, really okay." Chase's half smile didn't read as the confident smirk he so often wore, but something softer, maybe even as young as Tommy felt right then.

Emboldened, or perhaps just drunk on his first kiss, Tommy touched Chase's ear and cheekbone. "Okay enough for more?"

"Hell, yeah," Chase said. When he laughed into it with lips already open and breath warm against his skin, Tommy was surprised to learn that kissing could be many things. Kissing could be the kind of fun that was more than just feeling good and hormones, fun that was playful and so present in the moment.

He had just begun to lean back, swaying with the pressure from Chase's body, scattering cards carelessly, when they heard the slam of the screen door.

"Oh, shit! God, sorry, *sorry*." Cheryl covered her eyes and spun around.

"Relax, everyone is dressed," Chase said.

Mortified, Tommy buried his face in his hands. His cheeks blazed hot against cold palms.

"I'm just...we're going to go back. Yeah." Tommy peeked up in time to see Jake peeking over her shoulder, smiling way too wide and giving Chase the most unsubtle thumbs up of all time.

"Oh, well—"

"Sounds great. Shoo," Chase said before Tommy could demur politely.

"Oh, my god." Tommy said when the door closed behind them.

"Come on." Chase stood and tugged on the shoulder of Tommy's sleeve. "Wanna go to my room? It's more private."

Holy shit. Okay. This was happening. Tommy took a breath. He wanted more privacy, he wanted to die of mortification, and he had no idea how to ask for more kisses even when he knew he really wasn't ready for a lot of stuff that "privacy" implied. Still, he let Chase catch his hand and followed him into his room. It was a mess, with clothes on literally every surface, down to a shirt hanging from a lampshade. Most of the sheets and the blanket had slid onto the floor. The windows were cracked, which was the source of the hollow, eerie whistle of wind he'd been hearing all along. It was chilly. Chase sat on the bed, and so did Tommy. He couldn't forget, though, Cheryl's knowing smile and Jake's thumbs up. What the hell was he doing here with a gorgeous guy who probably knew what he was doing?

"Hey, it's cool," Chase said, pulling Tommy's hands from his face. "It's not the end of the world. Haven't you ever been caught—"

"Oh, um. Well, no." Tommy took a breath. "You'd have to have been…kissing someone. For that."

"Tommy." Chase's smile split his face, so he looked younger, infinitely more vulnerable and open. "Was that your first kiss?"

"Is it completely embarrassing if I say it was?"

"Uh, no." Chase fist pumped the air. "Score team Chase."

"Score?" Tommy tried to control his face.

"No, no, not like that." Chase scooted back until he was propped against the wall. "I mean like…this is really nice. I'm excited and…honored. Oh, my god, that's so cheesy isn't it?"

"No," Tommy said. A smile rose from his toes to his fingers and seeped through to his lips. "Well, maybe. A little. But not in a bad way."

"You only get to be someone's first kiss once. If ever. That's pretty awesome."

"Have you been someone else's?" Emboldened, Tommy put his hand on Chase's knee.

"No." Chase rolled his eyes. "I know I come off confident and all. I'm told it's kind of annoying sometimes. But I've only ever kissed one other person."

Tommy started to speak but bit back his questions.

"How'd someone like you go so long with no kisses?" Chase asked.

"I go to a small Catholic school. We've all known each other for years. I mean, there could be another gay kid at my school, but, if there is, I don't know. It would be weird anyway."

"I can see that."

"But wait," Tommy said as he turned toward Chase. "What do you mean, someone like me?"

Chase traced the backs of Tommy's fingers. Tommy twitched under the soft touch. "You know how cute you are, right?"

Tommy wrinkled his nose. "Cute?"

"As in, good looking. And just—" Chase waved a hand, as if to encompass all of him. "Just *you*. I like everything about you."

"Uh." Tommy cleared his throat. "Something must be wrong with you then. Because all of me includes the weird parts. Like when I say the wrong thing, which is ninety percent of my conversation. And man, I'm so awkward. I mean, yesterday I tripped over nothing at all and have sand burns on both knees."

Chase kissed below Tommy's earlobe and spoke against his skin. "That's part of it," he said. Heat flooded Tommy's body, and he marveled that such a small thing, just one kiss, could make his whole body light up. "It's endearing."

When Chase swayed against him, Tommy let himself be pressed back until he was on his back with Chase propped up next to him. Chase's hair hung down around his face. Tommy wanted so, so much, to learn if his hair was as silky as it looked and what Chase's lips might look like after endless kisses and if Chase would feel the electricity of a simple kiss to his neck. Tommy thought maybe, with Chase's gold-lit eyes unwavering, he could see what Chase would look like if Tommy kissed his neck—if he was brave enough.

Tommy figured he could be that brave. But he was also uncomfortable, contorted with his legs hanging off the bed, and completely unsure of what the boundaries were, or how to set them.

"Take your shoes off," Chase said, kicking off his own flip-flops and scooting up until he was lying on his side. Tommy did and lay down, too. Emboldened by Chase's smile and how comfortable he seemed, Tommy scooted until there was barely any room between them, just enough to feel the electric charge of potential running hot, sparking between their bodies. He put his hand on Chase's hip. His index finger slipped under Chase's shirt accidentally.

"Chase," Tommy said. He licked his lips; his nerves buzzed even louder than desire. "I...I don't know what I'm doing and I don't want to make you think I'm—"

"Tommy. Can I kiss you? I promise, there's no pressure. I'd say I am cool with anything you want, but...*I'm* not. I mean, I'm not ready for more than that really."

Tommy sighed and smiled with his whole body. Chase trailed a touch from the knob of his wrist, over his forearm, and around his bicep. "You can definitely kiss me. A lot."

WHEN HE WAS ALONE IN his bed that night, Tommy mulled over the things he'd learned. How simple touches could make his body sing. How he had the power to make a good-looking, confident boy turn to putty when he sucked lightly along his collarbone. He was delighted to find out, after several kisses, each their own experiment in what worked best, that a sharp nip to his bottom lip could be very, very dangerous. Should future Tommy ever get to make out with a kind, beautiful boy again, he'd try to remember long division the moment he was kissed like that again.

CHAPTER FIVE

TOMMY AWOKE THE NEXT MORNING to silence; the wind must have died down, thank god. At first, the constant whistle of air and the buffeting noise of wind burst had been cool, atmospheric. After a few days, it felt as if his ears had been assaulted. Now hey rang in the silence left by the absence of wind.

It was his last day. Tomorrow was the long drive back home to his normal life, away from what felt like the first time he'd ever really been awake. Tommy smiled at his own melodrama and ran his fingers over the sensitive skin of his stomach. He only had a few weeks until his life would change again, until *past* Tommy would have to dive into a completely different world, forced to become *future* Tommy. He would never admit this to anyone, but he was to-the-bones-terrified of what was to come. Or, well, he'd never admitted it *before.* Until this moment he hadn't even let himself wallow to trace the shape of his fear.

Maybe he could admit it now because he woke up a completely different person, someone who had been kissed, who really, really understood how hungry his body could be, how greedy he could feel for more and more. If allowed, Tommy could gladly kiss Chase (and maybe more) every day for weeks.

His stomach dropped, the fluttering of remembered arousal free-fell into anxiety. Why did he kiss Chase anyway? Aside from the obvious. Because the truth was that there was an even bigger obvious. They'd started something that could never go anywhere. A deep insecurity had always been sewn into him that he would never be desirable, that he'd never get a first kiss, much less a second. He'd never have someone hold his hand or get a casual kiss hello and a longer kiss goodbye and everything that came after those kisses. And those were all things he and Chase could never give each other. Chase had already had those kisses with someone else.

Another lesson learned: Tommy wasn't made for casual. Kisses were nice (okay, amazing), but he wanted…a boyfriend.

"Tommy?" His mother tapped on the door. "You up yet, honey?"

He huffed. "I am now." A glance at his phone told him it was 11:30, which he conceded was a little late. He had been up anyway.

"Well, lunch is ready if you want some sort of first meal of the day."

He pulled on basketball shorts and a clean shirt. She was still hovering by the door when he emerged. She ruffled his hair and smiled with a fondness he thought was maybe edged with something else: longing, wistfulness. They didn't talk about it much, but he knew she wasn't ready for him to go either.

"Sorry. I guess I was tired."

"I guess that happens when you stay out 'til one in the morning with friends you've only just met."

"Mom—"

"I'm kidding, honey," she said. He shuffled past her. The kitchen table was loaded with leftovers: reheated pasta, some ribs, coleslaw, and a buffet of sandwich makings. He grabbed some of everything, kissed her cheek in thanks, and made his way to the screened-in porch. The bright sun played over the water; skittering clouds spilled inky blue over the lake's otherwise-variegated shades, sapphire to periwinkle.

Laughter spilled across the lawns. A couple of Chase's younger cousins were crammed onto a low wooden swing and shouting the words to a repetitive song, changing the lyrics from time to time and cracking each other up. An impromptu soccer game seemed to be going on.

"It's going to be a beautiful day." His mom joined him on the porch. Her fingers were wrapped around a glass of iced tea. "Thank god. I think maybe this was the worst beach vacation we've ever had."

"Oh, I don't know," Tommy said carelessly. "It's been pretty awesome."

"Oh, has it?" Her glass clinked when she set it on the table. "Wanna talk about it?"

Tommy blushed so hard, so suddenly, he surprised even himself. "No. I don't know." They'd never had a conversation like this. Jerry had done the sex talk thing, which had been agonizing, not because they didn't have a good relationship, but because he'd admittedly had no idea how to talk about sex that wasn't of the hetero variety and Tommy had ended up having to talk him through it.

"It's the strangest thing, you know," she said. Her eyes were on the horizon. "Knowing that, in a few weeks, you're going to have a life that I'll know nothing about."

"That's not true," Tommy said. Her lips were pressed together; he made that face, too, whenever he was trying to control a deep emotion. "I'll still come home and call. I'm not leaving forever or anything."

"Oh, honey. But you are. It won't ever be the same."

"True." He took her hand. From his bones to his heart, he knew then exactly what she meant. Growing up with her, having her around for him whenever he wanted, he'd taken that for granted. Soon, she'd only know the pieces of him he chose to share. And it would be so easy to drift away. Tommy swallowed. Maybe it would be best to start figuring out how to create new bridges now, so it wouldn't be too hard when he was gone. "Wanna know something?"

"Yes." She squeezed his hand.

"Chase kissed me last night." Telling her wasn't as hard as he'd thought it might be.

"First kiss?" Her smile lit up her face.

"Yeah." Tommy bit his lip. "And it was…" She waited him out, even when his hand slipped from hers. He traced the wooden grain of the table. "Amazing,"

"That's wonderful. Really. I wish—" She broke off with a little laugh.

"What?"

"My first kiss was so awful. It was awkward and…well, *bad*." She winked at him. "A good first kiss is something for the books, honey."

Dreamily, he remembered how his heart had pounded so hard it hurt, his surprise, and his acquiescence to pleasure. "But I'll never see him again." The acknowledgement hit like whiplash.

"That's hard. But, Tommy." His mother met his eyes. "It'll be a good memory, right? You'll always have that."

He smiled. "Definitely."

They sat in silence. Idly, he watched as Ethan scored a goal and the adults sitting around the game cheered.

"Thanks, Mom," he said finally. "For talking to me. Like this."

"No, honey." She stood and cupped his cheek, then kissed his forehead. "Thank you for sharing that with me."

HALF AN HOUR LATER HANNAH and Ethan wandered over, asking to go down to the water.

"I can take them," he told his mom.

"It's so nice, let's all go down." She was slathering Ethan with sunscreen. "Would you mind getting that lounge chair out of storage for me?"

"Uh, sure." Tommy grabbed sunglasses and worked his way down to the shed that was under their deck. Truth be told, he did mind, because it was damp and gross. Earwigs and spiders loved it in there, also, occasionally, toads. Not that he minded any of those so much individually, but he wasn't a fan of all of them all at once, skittering out and from under things unexpectedly. He wrestled the chair down and settled it in a patch of shade that he knew would be sunny once the sun broke over the tall trees behind their cottage. Last night, Hannah and Ethan had dug a giant hole in the sand right by the volleyball net, which seemed like an accident in the making. With a sigh, he settled in the sand and slowly filled it in.

"What's this, early morning labor?"

Tommy's head popped up at the sound of Chase's voice. "More like afternoon labor."

Chase sat next to him. "True. I only just woke up, so it's morning to me."

"Same." Tommy ran his fingers through the sand. "I figured if anyone wanted to play volleyball, this looked like a broken leg, at minimum. I'm guessing my siblings are responsible."

"Naw." Chase began shoveling the sand. "All the kids were involved."

Tommy paused to look Chase over. His cheeks were a little pink, and the smile he tossed at Tommy was bright, but a bit uncertain.

"Morning," Tommy said softly.

"Afternoon," Chase said.

Tommy jostled him with his shoulder. "It's a time of day." he bit his lip and gathered courage. "I'm happy to see you, no matter what time it is."

Chase stopped shoveling and leaned closer. Tommy had a split second to marvel at his own daring; he was about to kiss a boy in broad daylight on a beach. Jake's voice startled them.

"Chase, c'mon we gotta go to the store."

"Ugh," Chase hung his head. "I forgot."

Tommy sat back and took a breath. *What had gotten into him?* "Everything okay?"

Chase stood, brushed sand off of his legs, and pulled Tommy up by the hand. He squeezed his fingers. "Definitely." Tommy knew he meant more than just this moment, and that settled him. Rationally, he knew last night had been awesome. Irrationally, his insecurity whispered that maybe Chase hadn't liked it or him.

"Listen," Chase said, glancing back over his shoulder. "We gotta run to town for food and supplies and stuff. But we're having a bonfire tonight. Do you wanna come? Your family is invited and all. S'mores all around."

"Yeah, I'd love that." Tommy swallowed. "I mean, I'll ask them. But I would like to."

"Awesome. We'll probably hang out, too, after the kids go to bed. My uncle bought a crazy amount of fireworks. I think they're all gonna get a bit crazy tonight. My parents letting loose? I can't even."

Tommy had no idea what qualified as letting loose, but he nodded.

"We're gonna hang out down here, Jake and Cheryl and I. Would you stay for that, too? Please."

"Definitely." There was no other answer he could or would give. "We might do some family game night stuff before the kids go to bed, but I'll come down after?"

"*Chase.*" Jake jingled car keys; his voice was sharp.

"Coming!" He turned back to Tommy, surprising him with a kiss on his cheek. "See ya."

TOMMY EXPECTED MORE PUSHBACK WHEN he announced his intention to go to the bonfire. He didn't ask, which was new. It wasn't even three days ago that his mother had pushed back, hard, when he'd tried to do something on his own. His mom smiled, and Tommy knew then that they were both coming to terms with the fact that he was moving on soon.

"Okay," she said, taking the cards from him and storing them in the cupboard where they kept their games and books.

"Don't be out too late though," Jerry said. "We're gonna have a lot to do in the morning to get on the road by eleven."

"Can do." Tommy executed a sloppy salute and drank in their smiles.

THAT NIGHT, TOMMY SAT IDLY burning a marshmallow, allowing it to catch fire before blowing out the soft halo of blue and yellow flames. Chase bumped his shoulder.

"So, you're a burning-your-marshmallow kind of guy, huh?"

The sun clung to the horizon. Dark pressed in from the east. The stars were disrobing, one by one, and Chase's face in gloaming, a study of shadows cast by the fire, was painfully beautiful. Nightfall and one final stolen moment on a beach were all Tommy had right now. He wanted desperately to kiss Chase, even in front of Jake and Cheryl. He would, if only he thought he could stand it. *How are you doing this so easily?*

"Watch," he said instead. Balancing a graham cracker on his knee, he pulled on the skin of crisped marshmallow, slipping it off of the molten core. Juggling the roasting stick, still with marshmallow on it, he made a s'more out of the shell. "And now, you can make another." He held what was left of the marshmallow over the bonfire. The flames were snapping now, leaping toward the night.

"But it's burned." Chase wrinkled his nose.

"It's toasted." Tommy handed the s'more to him. "Try it. It's good."

"If you say so," Chase said, with a shake of his head and a tiny slip of laughter.

"It's an art, you see." Tommy explained. "You have to let it catch fire, but just a little. Control it." He swallowed a sudden tightness in this throat. Is that what he was doing?

"And that's it? It's done then?"

It had to be; Tommy knew that. Chase had given him something to carry for the rest of his life. Bittersweet, a kiss lingered, a haunting, delicious memory that made his lips tingle. He wanted more; he was hungry in a way he'd never realized he could be. How could he have known desire would be hunger pangs rather than appetite, empty palms and the aching throb of blood under his skin? This was *real*, this what daydreams meant.

"No," Tommy said.

Chase was gamely taking a bite. Tommy liked the thoughtful look on Chase's face as he gave it a shot. "Sorry, man, I don't think I'm a fan."

"You don't have to be," Tommy said quietly. Chase's eyes pierced his, unblinking, pooled in darkness.

"Tommy—"

"That's not all," Tommy rushed. "You do it again. It's kind of a game, see. How many times can you get one layer off? Can you get it just right each time?"

"Can you?" Chase handed him the uneaten half of his s'more. Contrary to Tommy's directions, what marshmallow had been on his stick was being burnt into oblivion. Tommy laid the stick on the sand and considered the multitude of responses that burned on his tongue and the back of his throat. They were past subtext now and they both knew it.

"I've never managed." The graham cracker crumbled, scattering onto his pants, into the wind, lost in the dun and tan of the sand. No one would ever know it had been there, come morning.

"You wanna go for a walk?" Chase spoke quietly, just a whisper over the chatter of friends around the fire and the raucous laughter of his parents and aunts and uncles on the deck. It was the last night, and the last night always went like this: his family preparing quietly to leave, packing and putting to rest the game that was vacation. Routine would rise with the sun as surely as the last bit of summer freedom had set. The others—those renting cottages around them, regardless of the roving groups and families each year—turned this last night into revelry. Tommy had seen and heard it all: midnight games of tag, drunken laughter over country music blasting from a stereo, fireworks, firecrackers, fights. Any other year he'd be packed; he'd be in his bed with his windows open to catch the last sounds of water, to listen to the last vestiges of summer, and imagining what it might be like to not have to slip into his homebound skin.

Soon, Tommy would shed that skin. Home would mean the place he lived most. Who would he be every time he changed into Tommy-coming-to-visit?

The most sobering thought: What if nothing really changed? What if he was the same tired, isolated version of himself wherever he went for the rest of his life? Last night, Chase had opened a door, had introduced him to his body, a foreign self that was unbearably sensitive, beautiful in its potential for pleasure, and helplessly entranced by the freedom of letting go.

Through the night, Tommy had pressed his fingers to each spot Chase had kissed, had tried to force the memories in and in, so he'd never forget even if he may one day regret them. Beyond the circle of butter-colored firelight was the deep dark of places outside the city, where the scattering of stars was a brilliant blanket of lights. Tommy remembered Chase's lips behind his ear and thought, *yes*.

Beyond the circle of light, Chase caught Tommy's pinky with his own, curling them together. "Could I hold your hand?"

"Yeah," Tommy said, caught off guard by the uncharacteristic uncertainty.

"So…" Chase watched the ground beneath their feet and tugged on Tommy's hand when they came to driftwood they needed to step over. Most of the cottages were dark. It was pushing eleven. Even the sounds of the beach party were faded and the wind and the water made their constant presence known. "Was last night—did I, like, pressure you, or was it not good or—"

"Oh, no, god." Tommy couldn't read Chase's face. "No, I wanted it. To." He cleared his throat.

"But you regret it." Chase said. Tommy pulled him to a stop. Dune grass whispered when the wind kicked up.

"No. Well, not exactly." Rueful and a little sad, he tested words in his mind, trying to get them just right. "I don't regret last night with you. It was amazing. You were."

"Yeah?" Chase shifted closer.

Everything was so heavy all at once. His anxieties and his fears felt like stones pressing him into the wet sand. He'd never felt gravity like this. Tommy shrugged and took a deep breath and thought, *but this is here. This is wanting. And I want.*

And so, on his toes, heart pounding so hard it drowned the beach song around them, he kissed Chase.

"Seriously," he said against Chase's wet lips when he pulled away.

"Amazing," Chase agreed. "But it's not a controlled burn. Is that it? The part that scares you?"

Tommy inhaled sharply. "I'm pretty obvious, aren't I?"

"No," Chase said. He, too, considered his words. "You were just…there, but not, tonight. So different from last night, and

I thought maybe it was because you regretted it, or I had gone too far or something. But then—"

"You're turning my marshmallow into a metaphor?" Tommy laughed, incredulity painting the words. His skin pebbled with cold in the wind. Chase rubbed his arms to warm him. Tommy tilted his head left.

"Wanna sit?" A few yards from the water was a little alcove of beach, protected by dune grass and flowers. They settled, this time closer, touching from shoulders to knees, and with their intertwined fingers on Chase's lap. He traced the curves of Tommy's nail beds. It wasn't a sensual touch and yet it shivered its way up Tommy's spine.

"You just seem so sure," Tommy said at last.

"About kissing you?"

"No, just…everything. When you were talking about college. You're leaving. Like, *leaving*. You're going to be an airplane ride away." Tommy took a deep breath. "And here I am, scared to go less than an hour from home."

"What are you scared of?" Chase asked.

"I guess I always thought college would be, like, this place where I could try to be someone…different. I mean, me but…a new me."

"What kind of *new me*? You're kind of mind-blowing as is." Chase's lips on his cheek were smiling, and that Tommy could know this in the dark was thrilling.

"I don't know. I'm…I'm always responsible, I always try to be good. I kinda always told myself it's what I wanted. But the closer it gets, I think, really, I'm scared. I've been scared."

"I mean…I'm scared. I know I come off as confident, but right now…" Tommy waited him out, giving Chase the space to find the right words. "We're told, like, *all the time*, how big of a deal this is. At least, I always was."

"You mean the 'what you choose now will determine the rest of your life' speech?"

"Yeah, man. And like, all the time. Taking the PSAT? 'Sleep well and eat because this is one of the first steps to the rest of your life.'"

"Taking the ACT? 'Everything hinges on this single moment,'" Tommy added.

Chase snorted a laugh. "'Choose the right college.' 'This is the biggest decision you'll ever make.'" The words were dry, laced with a hard edge. Almost bitter. "I dunno. Do you ever thing it's just crap?"

"Choosing the right college?" He couldn't clearly see Chase, but confused, he still tried to read his face.

"Yeah. Like, I don't know how to make fuckin' mac 'n cheese! Seriously. Who put me in charge of this?" Chase put his head on Tommy's shoulder. "I think—well, hope—we can change our minds, if we need to. There's all this pressure to get this one choice right, when we have no idea what it's even like to be on our own."

"So…what you're saying is that nothing is set in stone," Tommy hazarded.

"Maybe. Maybe that's just one part of it." Chase shifted, then lay down and tugged Tommy with him. "God, look at the stars."

"I know." Tommy thought he'd always remember this. He thought of bittersweetness and how it lingered. How, after he'd left Chase's room last night, he'd tried to control the swell of emotions tangling in his chest and belly and heart. No one wanted to be hurt, and Tommy was terrified that he'd walk away from an amazing memory and regret it. "I'm scared of not having control," Tommy confessed. He rolled toward Chase. They'd be covered in sand, and the damp was seeping into his clothes. A chill was settling into his bones, but Chase was so warm.

"I get that," Chase said. "But there's only so much you can control. No matter how much you want to know how something will end."

"Like this," Tommy said. He held his breath, wondering at how the words sounded, how they might land. There was such a gap between intention and reception. Even words, he realized, were out of his grasp the moment he loosed them. Suddenly he knew. He felt his body at a precipice, on the edge of something huge, and had no idea what would be there when he tipped forward.

"No." Chase traced Tommy's nose and then lips with a gentle finger. "That doesn't mean meeting you wasn't awesome."

They would never have this again. Sure, they could keep in touch, trade funny snaps chronicling transitions into dorms and parties and classwork. Perhaps this fleeting connection would fade. Perhaps they'd become the sort of friends with a shared memory but nothing else in common. They were bound for different lives, different states, different truths. Tommy couldn't begin to guess how that was going to feel a week, a month, years from now. Maybe it would hurt; he was sure that at first it would. It stung already. A goodbye sat on the horizon, ready to rise with the sun.

The electric shock of Chase's lips on his, right then, in the whisper of wind and the honesty of August in Michigan, the smell of sand dunes and late summer flowers, stripped him. He opened his lips to Chase's. His fingers were lined with sand he scattered through Chase's hair. Tommy let Chase press him back onto the sand. There was nothing about this night he wouldn't remember, and *that*—that was a beautiful thing. The unknown lingered. This was a moment he could never have predicted, and maybe he felt a little wild, and maybe he was giving in to a recklessness that was utterly unlike him, but, deep down, Tommy trusted that it would be okay. He trusted that he'd be okay and that maybe change would mean holding on to who he was deep down but letting go a little as well, letting himself take a chance.

Chance was a risk, but everything, everything that was coming next was, too, no matter how much Tommy had wanted to control it. He risked his heart with Chase, and not because he thought this was love. It was because he was putting himself into someone else's hands. He was taking a piece of Chase for himself as well and that—when they exchanged little pieces of themselves—was a moment Tommy would always remember and think *That was the moment when I let myself be.*

ABOUT JUDE SIERRA: Jude Sierra is a Latinx poet, author, academic and mother working toward her PhD in Writing and Rhetoric, looking at the intersections of Queer, Feminist and Pop Culture Studies. Her novels include *A Tiny Piece of Something Greater* (Foreword INDIES Finalist, 2019), *What it Takes* (Starred Review, *Publishers Weekly*), and *Idlewild*, a contemporary LGBTQ romance set in Detroit's renaissance that was named one of *Kirkus Reviews'* Best Books of 2016.

LOVE IN THE TIME OF COFFEE

by Kate Fierro

0. BEFORE COFFEE

GEMMA WAS REALLY HUNGRY.

The meeting at the school had been fun, just as Mom had promised. It was nice to play with other kids, and the teacher, Miss Lily, was pretty and smiled all the time. She could draw funny animals, too. Gemma was glad Miss Lily would be their teacher when they all started school in the fall.

But they had been here so very long. She was not used to being around so many people all at once. It was loud, everyone talked and moved all the time, and, after a while, even the most interesting games couldn't hold Gemma's attention. She just wanted to hide in some quiet corner and have a nap, even though naps were for babies.

She was also hungry. The carrots and celery sticks Mom brought for her were long gone, and Gemma was not allowed to eat any of the snacks and cookies laid out on the table in the big room. She had watched other kids stuff their faces with the sweet treats and sat on her hands so as not to reach for one. Those were bad for you, Mom said. She promised, if Gemma was good, she would get a special treat for lunch: her favorite buckwheat pancakes with blackberries and coconut yogurt that she only got on special occasions.

And she *had* been good. She hadn't cried or made a fuss, she'd sat quietly on a chair waiting for the adults to finish their meeting, and she hadn't taken a single little cookie for all the eleventy hours they had been here. But now her tummy ached, and she really wanted to go home, and her mom was still standing in the big room talking to three other ladies, even though almost everybody else had left already. Gemma squeezed her eyes shut. She was a big girl now. Big enough to start school soon. Big girls didn't cry.

"Yes, I agree it all sounds lovely," her mom said. "The only concern I have is the food. I'm pleasantly surprised with the dairy-free and vegan options, but the menu we've been shown still leaves a lot of questions. Are all of the meals made fresh every day? What about the quality of the ingredients? I just feel the principal should be able to tell us whether they use organic or local products, and what is the school's stand on GMO and preservatives in the food they serve to our children."

After a moment of silence, Gemma opened her eyes, hoping it was finally time to go home. But the other ladies were just looking at her mom with funny faces. Then one shook her head, which made her long, black hair dance prettily.

"Well, judging by the quality of coffee they've served today, I'd say we have nothing to worry about." She drank from a paper cup in her hand, smiling. There was a dimple in her brown cheek.

Gemma's mom huffed, the way she did every time Gemma said something silly. "Please. A high-quality poison isn't any less harmful. Did you know that coffee is one of the worst substances you can put in your body, right next to sugar? In fact—"

Gemma sighed. When Mom started to talk about food, it was ages before she stopped. She rubbed her eyes and looked around at the snack table. Maybe there was something there that wasn't *very* bad? But all the plates were empty, with only crumbs and a few juice spills remaining. She wriggled on the chair, dangerously close to tears.

"Hi, what's your name?"

Gemma whipped around, finding a girl on her other side, a short one, with light brown skin and very dark hair. Gemma remembered her from the music games. She had a very pretty voice.

The girl smiled widely, not waiting for Gemma's reply.

"Miss Lily said, but I forgot. It's rude to forget your friend's name, isn't it? Will you be my friend?" She squeezed Gemma's hand in her sticky one. "I'm Anya. Do you want to share a cookie with me? I saved the last one."

She let go of Gemma's hand and pulled a big, round chocolate cookie out of the kangaroo pocket in her pink hoodie. Gemma's eyes widened.

"I can't," she said, glancing at her mom.

"Why? Are you *arergic*? My cousin is *arergic* to peanut butter, and he can't eat peanut butter because he will die, and I think it's really sad. Will you die if you eat a cookie?"

Gemma shook her head. "No, but my mom says cookies are bad for health, so I can't have any."

Anya frowned at the cookie in her hand. "Really? They always make me feel good." She thought for a bit, then grinned. "You know, *my* mom says that if you really, really, *really* want something, then it's okay to have a little bit, even before dinner. So if you really, really, *really* want a cookie, you can share one with me, yes?"

Gemma looked at the adults still talking at the other side of the room and nodded. She'd never heard about that rule, but it made sense. She really, really, *really* wanted that cookie—even more than she wanted her pancakes right now.

Anya grabbed her hand and tugged. "Come on, it will be our *secret*!"

Gemma followed her to the room where they'd played the music games. It was empty now, quiet. She sat on one of the big pillows on the floor next to Anya and took the offered half of the cookie—the bigger piece, she noticed. It smelled like angels and unicorns.

"I'm Gemma," she said before taking a bite. "And I will be your *best* friend."

1. MOCHA

THE COFFEE SHOP WAS FILLED with chatter and the pleasant smell of freshly ground coffee. April sun streamed in through the large windows. With its simple décor in black and white and an assortment of seasonal drinks, it was the closest to trendy their little town had to offer. Gemma shifted nervously in the short line.

"Are you sure they will sell it to us?" she whispered, leaning closer to her best friend's ear.

Anya laughed. "Of course they will, silly, it's not alcohol."

"My mom says caffeine should be regulated too. That it should be illegal to sell caffeinated drinks to kids. Or pregnant women."

"Well, it's lucky we are neither, then." Anya grinned and pushed the long dark curtain of her hair over her shoulder. "Fifteen is hardly childhood. And I thought you didn't believe it would rot your brain."

"No, I know, but…" Gemma bit her lip; her heart beat fast. "I want to do this, but it's still scary, trying something you were lectured against all your life."

"I know." Anya squeezed Gemma's sweaty hand. "But I've never tried it either, remember? We're both coffee virgins."

Gemma gasped, her freckled cheeks burning. "You can't say things like that!"

Anya grinned, showing her small, even teeth. "It's true, though. This will be our first time." She waggled her eyebrows. "A true initiation."

Gemma hid her face behind her strawberry blond curls.

"What can I get you, girls?" The barista smiled at them. Anya stepped toward the counter.

"Two large mochas, please. With whipped cream."

"Coming right up. That's eight fifty."

Anya put the two crumpled fives on the counter. "Keep the change," she said breezily, as if she did this every day. Gemma looked at her with awe. If only she could find it in herself to be as cool and collected.

"He's cute," Anya murmured in her ear as soon as they stepped aside to wait for their drinks.

"Who?"

"The barista."

Gemma considered the boy as he took an order from another customer. He was young, maybe college-aged, short and compact, with a tousled mess of brown hair falling in his face. She didn't see the appeal, although he did have a nice smile.

Minutes later, they were sitting in velvet-covered armchairs by the little corner table, ready to take their first sip. The blue paper cup was pleasantly warm in Gemma's hands.

"We're doing this together, on three," Anya said. Her brown eyes were bright. "One. Two. *Three.*"

The mocha tasted lovely: smooth, cool whipped cream followed by the hot sweetness of milky coffee with just a hint of chocolate. Gemma swallowed the first sip, then immediately took another and closed her eyes in pleasure.

"Mmm," she hummed as she put down her cup. "It's much better than I thought."

Anya licked her lips with a little frown. "It's good, but awfully sweet. I think I'll have to try a latte next or a cappuccino."

Gemma grinned, raising the cup to her lips once more. "So we're doing this again?"

"Of course! Not too soon, though. I doubt our parents are going to give us a coffee budget even if we ask nicely."

Gemma laughed, feeling light and buoyant with a sudden burst of happiness. "My mom won't for sure. But we can save some money every now and then. It can be our special treat, just for the two of us together."

Anya picked up her cup with a brilliant smile. "I *love* that idea."

2. FRAPPE

THE STREET OUTSIDE THE COFFEE shop was deserted. The air shimmered in the July heat. Gemma took a sip of her blessedly cold mint frappe and looked at Anya from under the wide rim of her sun hat.

"So what's your big news? Are your parents buying you a car for your sweet sixteen after all?"

Anya laughed; the sound carried brightly in the still air. "I wish. No, but it's the next best thing."

"Which is?"

"I have a boyfriend!" Anya squealed and bounced a few times. Her iced latte sloshed dangerously.

"What?" Gemma exclaimed. "How? *Who?*"

"Ben." Anya pulled her by the hand to sit on the dusty steps of the library, where the roof offered a bit of shade.

"*Ben?* Trumpet-player-ponytail-never-talks-to-anyone Ben?"

"He's just shy."

"You never even told me you liked him!"

"I didn't want to jinx it." Anya's brown cheeks blossomed with a rare blush. "We've been chatting on Facebook for a couple of weeks now, and last night we went on our first date. Gem, it was *perfect.*"

Unable to contain her excitement, she jumped to her feet. Her sundress, a vivid splash of color against the heat-bleached street, danced around her muscular thighs as she paced. Gemma felt an unpleasant pang in her chest. Was it silly that she felt betrayed?

Yes, yes it was. She forced the little ball of hurt down and set her face into a look of interest.

"What did you do?"

"Oh, nothing much. We got coffee and then drove around in his car talking. And we parked in a field and watched the sunset."

Gemma tried her best to smile. "That must have been nice."

"It was. And then we made out for, like, two hours. It was *crazy.*"

"Anya!" Gemma nearly dropped her cup.

The grin on Anya's face was all delight; her eyes sparkled. "What? We were just kissing. He has the most incredible lips, you know? Must be all that trumpet practice. I never thought kissing could feel like that."

Incredulous, Gemma shook her head. "And he asked you to be his girlfriend?"

"When we were saying goodnight on my porch. I said yes, of course. I really like him."

Gemma put the straw in her mouth and took a few gulps, barely feeling the cold. "Wow," she said when she could no longer delay a reaction. "I... I can't believe you didn't tell me, you goose. This is huge!"

"I know, I know. I'm sorry. Are you mad?" Anya batted her long eyelashes with an adorable pout.

"Are you kidding? I'm happy for you."

"You're the best!" Anya pulled her up and into a hug and pressed a quick kiss to her cheek, and Gemma did her best to stifle the ugly feeling in her gut. She was happy for Anya. She *was.* It would just take a little bit of getting used to. That was all.

3. DRIP

"I STILL CAN'T BELIEVE YOUR parents let us drive to the cabin all by ourselves!" Gemma wiggled happily, stretching her too-long legs in the cramped space of the passenger seat as best she could. It was a beautiful Friday afternoon, their junior year was nearly over, and they had the whole weekend at the lake cabin to look forward to.

Anya's smile was mischievous even in profile. "To be honest, they think Ben is going with us as the responsible newly minted adult and second driver."

Gemma sat straighter. "Your parents let you take *Ben*?"

"Only because you were going. I had to promise I would be sleeping with you in their bedroom, and Ben would be alone in mine."

"No, but they let you bring your boyfriend, and you *didn't*?"

Anya shrugged. "I wanted some girl time. We haven't had any for weeks."

That was true, and Gemma missed their sleepovers and lazy weekends together more than she could express. Still, something seemed off.

"Is everything all right between you two?" she asked.

"Of course it is," Anya scoffed, not even glancing at her. "It's just, if Ben came, it would make you uncomfortable."

"Anya. I would be fine. You shouldn't—"

Anya didn't let her finish. "*And* he would expect me to sneak into his bed once you were asleep, and I don't want to. So really, it's fine. Girls' weekend!" she trilled, driving the car into a rest stop parking lot. "Okay, I really need to pee. And we should get coffee. Even a three-hour road trip isn't complete without a coffee break."

Gemma caught her hand before she could get out of the car, forcing Anya to face her at last. "Hey. He's not… pressuring you, is he?" she asked carefully.

Anya shook her head quickly. "No. I promise, he's not. It's just that we've been together for almost a year, and he's been suggesting going further, and I'm not ready for that. We just need to talk—we will, soon. But not this weekend, and not at the cabin where he might expect something to happen."

Gemma nodded slowly, only marginally relieved. "You would tell me if he was giving you trouble, wouldn't you?"

"Of course I would. But there's no trouble. Just, you know… growing pains." Anya rolled her eyes with that self-deprecating little smile she used so often. "Now, come on. Coffee."

The store was dark, with a neglected look that gave Gemma the creeps. Even the air smelled stale. The surly man behind the counter followed them with hungry eyes as they crossed the cramped space to the bathroom. Well, followed Anya and her feminine curves, really. Gemma's awkward, boyish looks never got any heads turned, thank goodness. She made sure the bathroom door was properly locked behind them and breathed a sigh of relief when Anya declared they'd take their coffee to go. She didn't want to spend any longer than she had to at this place.

The creepy man poured them tar-like coffee from the half-empty pot and shrugged when they asked for milk. Safely back in the car, Gemma added two packets of sugar to hers, but it didn't help; the coffee was strong and bitter, with a burnt aftertaste. Anya made a face over her own cup.

"Blech. How long did that pot sit there?" Then she quirked an eyebrow. "Hey, I just realized: we're in a scary movie cliché. Two pretty girls traveling alone, empty road, bad coffee at a rundown store, a cabin in the woods. All we need is either a serial killer or zombie beavers."

Gemma snorted. "Zombie beavers?"

"There's a movie about those; I'm not even kidding. I saw a trailer with Ben. He tried to get me to watch the whole thing, but, no thank you, I'll stick to comedies. I have enough to last us all weekend, by the way, even if the weather breaks."

"Unless we're interrupted by zombie beavers," Gemma added, barely able to suppress her giggles.

"Yeah, or serial killers. Are you done with that sad excuse for a coffee? We still have an hour to go."

No serial killers or zombie anything bothered them, and they watched two lighthearted movies, ate microwave popcorn, and sipped sparkling cider before crawling into bed—the big one in Anya's parents' bedroom.

"I did promise them, didn't I?" Anya grinned, flushed from a hot shower and sweetly sleepy in her pink footie pajamas. "Plus, the basic mistake they always make in scary movies is getting separated."

Anya fell asleep instantly, but Gemma lay awake for a long time, trying to get comfortable on the too-soft mattress. The night was utterly black outside; every little noise was scary in its foreignness. The woods creaked and rustled; the lapping of water sounded like someone rowing stealthily closer. Gemma's heart hammered in her chest.

Determined to stay rational, she turned her eyes to her best friend's face, relaxed in sleep. In the darkness, it was an elusive play of shadows: a soft curve of a cheek, a dark smudge of eyelashes. This close, she could smell the strawberry scent of Anya's body wash. Gemma thought back to their conversation at the store, so expertly diverted by Anya, and the fierce wave of protectiveness returned with an intensity that startled her. If Ben hurt her… Anya knew how to take care of herself, and Gemma was not a violent person, not by a long shot. But if anyone hurt Anya, they would live to regret it. Dearly.

In the still darkness, she reached across the pillow and took her best friend's hand, which was curled next to her face. Anya smiled in her sleep.

4. ESPRESSO

"If I read one more page, I'm gonna *die*." Anya flipped onto her back and pushed the book to the floor. She blinked owlishly at the ceiling. "We need coffee."

Gemma marked a place in her own notes and moved them to the side. "If we have coffee now, we won't be able to sleep at all."

"That's the point. We cram all we can tonight and then tomorrow we get plenty of sleep and go for the SATs both prepared *and* rested." Anya sat up and stretched. Her soft pajama top rode up to show a strip of smooth skin.

She looked soft, without the make-up she'd taken to wearing in the last year, with her hair in a messy bun on top of her head. Gemma always found her beautiful, but tonight it hit her harder than ever. She barely resisted reaching out to touch.

Startled by the intensity of the urge, Gemma cleared her suddenly dry throat and got to her feet.

Anya followed, stepping toward the bedroom door. "Come on, I have to show you the new espresso machine my parents bought."

They crept downstairs through the sleeping house, and soon the cozy, neat kitchen was filled with a warm aroma that Gemma had long come to associate with their time together. She never drank coffee with anyone else. Her mom, still the health freak, never allowed any at home.

"Nope. No milk, no sugar." Anya stopped her before Gemma had a chance to open the fridge. "It's a proper, quality espresso, and we're drinking it straight tonight."

Gemma frowned at the little cups, filled to the brim with black, steaming liquid topped with a layer of crema. "This looks bigger than an espresso."

"It's a double. We need a good strong shot of caffeine. Now, drink up."

Gemma obediently raised the cup to her lips. She shuddered at the first mouthful of the bitter drink. It wasn't bad, exactly, just so much more intense than she was used to, rich and complex without the softening taste of milk and sugar. She finished her cup in a few more swallows, following Anya's lead. Already she felt more awake, if only from the scent.

"Are you hungry?" Anya asked.

"Not really, are you?"

"Just a little. We should eat something anyway to keep our energy up. How about a banana? It's supposed to be great when you need to stay awake."

"Fine."

They ate in silence, leaning against the counter side by side with the tiled white floor cold against their bare feet. Gemma was only halfway finished when Anya murmured, "Do you wanna know a secret?" She turned to Gemma with a coy smile. "I'm going to lose my virginity after the prom."

Gemma nearly choked on a bite of banana. "You're *what*?"

Anya laughed and rolled her eyes. "Yes, it's the biggest cliché ever, I know. But it feels right. I'm ready, Ben's more than ready, and I kind of want it that way. An unforgettable night. I'm already on the pill, and Ben has booked us a hotel room for after the dance. It's gonna be perfect." She smiled dreamily, and Gemma crammed the rest of the banana into her mouth to avoid blurting out something she absolutely shouldn't. Her stomach felt like lead; all of the butterflies were gone.

Anya didn't even seem to notice her silence. "How about you and Patrick? Any plans like that, by any chance?" She grinned, waggling her beautifully shaped eyebrows.

Gemma swallowed and forced her voice out through her tightened throat. "I'm not going to prom with Patrick."

"What? Why not?"

"I, um, I broke up with him, actually. Last week."

Anya's eyes widened. "Oh, my god, why didn't you tell me? What happened? Are you all right?" She stepped closer. Her hand stroked Gemma's bare arm. Gemma's breath stuttered, but she forced it to even out.

"I'm fine, really. I just realized he's not my type. It wasn't going anywhere."

"But you've been together for six months!"

"And it only showed that no matter how much I try, he won't ever be my type." Gemma shrugged. "So I ended it."

"Do you want to talk about it?" Anya looked concerned, ready to comfort, to hug, to drop everything else and just be the best friend possible.

Gemma shook her head and ran her hand through her hair. She was still surprised when her fingers met air after just a few inches; she wasn't used to this change that came on the heels of all the others this past week and was perhaps the most visible symbol of it all.

"Thanks. Not yet, okay? Let's just get back to studying. We have to kill the SATs if we want a chance at those scholarships."

Anya nodded; her full lips were pinched with worry. "Okay. Whenever you want to talk, though, I'm here, okay?"

"I know. Thank you."

The saddest thing was, as much as Gemma wanted—*needed*—to talk about that whirlwind of a week, to have *somebody* know, a part of her wasn't certain she would ever tell Anya. How could she, without spilling the deepest, darkest truth? The thought of keeping secrets from her best friend left her feeling sick with guilt, but it was still better than losing Anya altogether.

It didn't stop her silly heart from stumbling when Anya squeezed her hand, still just a breath away, and said with that sweet, dimpled smile,

"And I *love* your new haircut. I would never brave such a radical change, but on you it looks gorgeous."

Gemma smiled and followed her back upstairs without a word.

5. PUMPKIN SPICE LATTE

Brandishing a travel mug, Anya rushed into Gemma's dorm room like a gust of wildly colorful wind.

"Pumpkin spice latte, extra shot of espresso, with a sprinkle of nutmeg on top. You're welcome."

"You're a goddess." Gemma moaned, pulling her into a tight, quick hug. Anya's cheeks were pink and cold, and her hair, braided into a crown, smelled deliciously like freshly ground coffee. She'd come straight from her shift at the on-campus Starbucks, where she happily spent every waking hour that wasn't filled with classes.

Anya slipped off her coat, kicked off her boots, and dropped them in the middle of the room as she tended to do. Gemma snorted and moved them to the designated area.

"You have no idea how much I envy you living in the dorm," Anya said, already elbow-deep in her spacious backpack. "My aunt is impossible. Curfew at ten. Lights out at eleven. No boys. Thank god your roommate's away. I need a decadent movie night with brownies, wine coolers, and cuddles, and I haven't seen you all week."

She emerged from her backpack with a bright smile and an armful of goodies and put them on the bedside table before climbing onto the neatly made bed. Gemma followed with her laptop and a fluffy blanket, ready for a lovely, long, unbearably platonic girls' night with her best friend.

It was three hours and four episodes of *Gilmore Girls* later that Anya turned to her in the cozy cocoon. She was so close in the narrow dorm bed that her breath, warm and chocolate-scented, tickled Gemma's lips.

"So did you manage to convince your mom to finance that Italian trip for you?" she asked. "The deadline is on Friday."

Gemma tore her eyes away from Anya's pink, plushy lips before it got weird. "Um, no. We're not really… on speaking terms right now, to be honest." Actually, being honest was what started their fight in the first place, so perhaps the whole honesty thing was overrated.

Anya's beautiful face fell. "Oh, no. So you're not going?" Her permanently cold hand found Gemma's under the blanket and squeezed it tight, stealing Gemma's breath for a second before she could answer.

"No, I am. Funny thing happened, you know? Do you remember my aunt Natasha?"

"The one your mom doesn't talk to?"

"Yeah. Well, she must have talked to her now, because Natasha called me yesterday to tell me she wants to sponsor my trip. Said it was in place of all the birthday gifts she'd missed."

"Huh. That is strange." Anya was rubbing her thumb over the top of Gemma's hand, seemingly without thought but distracting nonetheless. "Maybe they've made up?"

"What, like they've put aside twenty years of differences because I was being 'an ungrateful brat with no respect for traditions or social norms'? Yay for that, seriously."

Deep down, Gemma believed it was more than that. There was something about the way Natasha told her to just be herself—twice, all earnest and intense. She even said Gemma could call her with anything she needed, anything at all, as if she knew what confession caused the new rift between Gemma and her mom and wanted to tell her she was on her side without forcing Gemma to talk about the topic. It seemed almost as if Natasha knew *exactly* how it was.

No, that wasn't possible.

"Well, what matters is that you're coming, right?" Anya grinned and cuddled closer until her head rested on Gemma's bony shoulder. That couldn't be comfortable, but she looked content with the new position. "Let your mom have her reunion with her sister all she wants. We are spending our spring break in *Italy*, thank you very much. Oh, my god, I can't wait to try Italian coffee! They say it's an orgasm for your taste buds."

Gemma could feel her stupid, pale skin burn with a blush.

"Yeah." She swallowed. "Yes, I'm sure it will be delightful."

6. CAFFÈ MAROCCHINO

"Ooooh, my god, this is amazing. This is the best coffee *ever*. It's like this coffee is my soulmate. I want to drink it every single day of my life."

The coffee was definitely interesting: rich espresso with some cocoa powder and a layer of milk foam, generously sprinkled with more cocoa. It was too bitter for Gemma, but a perfect match for Anya, as evidenced by her indecent moans that made Gemma's heart do funny things in her chest. Her eyes kept coming back to Anya's mouth, which was smeared with the Nutella that covered the sides of the glass. Her lips were pink and plump, and would probably taste all sweet, and—Gemma really needed to stop thinking about that.

Half the magic of the coffee was probably the location: a lovely little ristorante in a narrow side street in the middle of Rome. The building it occupied—a worn, yellow two-story house with laundry hung out to dry from the upper windows—was probably older than any building Gemma had ever visited back home. The two of them were seated outside, at a table covered with red-checkered cloth. A slight wind moved the strands of ivy hanging down from the wooden awning. All around them, people chattered in melodic Italian, and not understanding a word of it made Gemma feel deliciously as though she was surrounded by secrets and mystery.

It was warm for early March. The bright sun stirred something wild and joyous in Gemma's soul, and, oh, she could live like this forever, traveling the world, visiting all the places, breathing the history, and surrounding herself with different cultures and people and languages. She'd never been outside of the United States. She'd had no idea how *free* she would feel here, as if she could have anything she dreamed of, shape her life in any way she wanted.

She wondered if Anya would run away with her, if Gemma asked her to.

She would never ask her, in case the answer was no.

Anya took another sip of the Marocchino. She seemed right at home, with her colorful dresses and her bright laughter and her beautiful curves. Even the Italian language came easily to her, and three days into their stay, she was already using basic, everyday phrases in a way that sounded completely natural.

"I'm serious, Gem." She closed her eyes. "I could marry this coffee. If marriages between people and beverages were a thing, I would be on my knee right now."

Before Gemma could recover from that picture enough to form a response, Anya's eyes shot open. She put down the glass and leaned closer to Gemma. Bumped with a knee, the table wobbled.

"Oh, speaking of marriage: I think Ben is going to propose!"

All thoughts of traveling and the otherworldly beauty of her best friend under the Italian sun flew from Gemma's mind. "Wha— What?"

"When we were video chatting, he told me he wants to talk. Said he'd come to visit when I'm back, that this is a conversation we need to have in person."

"And you're sure it's *that*?" The fettuccine Gemma had eaten for lunch weighed heavily in her stomach.

Anya grinned. "What else could it be? He looked all cute and shy when he talked about it and he never gets shy anymore unless it's an important moment. And we'd talked about this, you know? Over the summer, before I left for college. About getting married one day."

Gemma's throat was closing up. She swallowed with difficulty and tightened a hand over the edge of her chair for an anchor. "But you're only nineteen."

Anya shrugged. "Well, we wouldn't go through with it right away, I'm sure. Not until I'm twenty-one at least. I intend to drink legally at my own wedding, thank you very much." She laughed—so bright, so happy, with the dimples Gemma loved so much. "And I think long engagements are romantic, don't you?"

"I… honestly never thought about it," Gemma croaked. She hoped her devastation wasn't coming through loud and clear. "So, you'll say yes, then? If he asks?"

Anya frowned. "Well, of course. What else would I say?"

"I don't know, do I? Which is why I asked. Because, well. It's such a big step, engagement; it's like promising forever. Forever with Ben, all your life, is… is that what you want?"

She was babbling. She needed to stop, because Anya was looking at her with confusion.

"He's a good man, Gem. We're good together."

Yes, but is it all you want from life? Just getting married to the first boyfriend you've ever had, never trying other people, other choices?

She wisely clamped her lips closed before any of that could escape; that would be unfair—to Anya and to Ben. So she just nodded.

Anya beamed at her again, clearly reassured.

"You'll be my maid of honor, right? I can't think of anybody else I'd rather have by my side at that special moment. You've always been my closest person in the whole world. I can't do it without you."

Gemma's breath caught at the unintended double meaning. She'd thought about it once, about Anya getting married—just once, because she wasn't a masochist. She'd visualized herself at Anya's side in a different role, not standing right there as Anya swore her love and loyalty to another; feeling that door close with every word the happy couple said; helping the girl she loved prepare for that special day when every little detail was lovingly chosen for her union with somebody else.

Even the thought of Anya getting married was like a knife to the heart. How would she ever survive actually being there?

And then she thought of *not* being there at all, of leaving that space—in the church and in Anya's life—empty.

She couldn't do it.

"Of course I'll be your maid of honor," she said with a smile that cost her more than anything ever had. "I love you. I wouldn't miss it for the world."

7. IRISH COFFEE

"Anya, sweetie, I don't think we should have another round. There's a *lot* of whiskey in this—"

"Shh." Anya put a cold finger on Gemma's lips, effectively cutting her off. "I'm moping here. And if I can mope with both coffee *and* liquor, I shall do just that."

Gemma nodded and watched Anya order the third round of Irish coffees from the nice tattooed bartender who used to work with her at Starbucks before moving on to this cozy little bar. He hadn't even mentioned their IDs.

The place wasn't crowded on a Monday night with only a few groups of people occupying the larger tables toward the back and clearly celebrating something. Their laughter was in stark contrast to the somber mood at their tiny table, secluded in the corner.

Gemma had already resigned herself to the prospect of Anya getting royally drunk and staying the night at the dorm with her. There was no way she could go home to her aunt like this. But that was fine. It wouldn't be the first night they spent together in Gemma's narrow bed.

It was getting Anya to the dorm that worried her. Gemma seemed to handle liquor better, the few times that they drank, but she felt a bit fuzzy around the edges already. Walking her inebriated and emotional best friend all the way across town was going to be a challenge.

"I mean, I get it, long distance is hard," Anya picked up her rant once she had a warm glass between her palms again. "It's been hard for me too, but you don't see *me* sleeping around. And he could have just *said* something. We could have found a way to see each other more often, or have Skype sex maybe, or phone sex, I don't know, *something*. And to think I was so sure he wanted to propose." She snorted into her glass, then her lips trembled, curling into that sad little moue of heartbreak. "I loved him, dammit," she mumbled.

Gemma dove into her coffee; the hot liquid burned her throat when she swallowed too much too fast. She was here as a *friend*. A good friend wouldn't utter any of the comments pinging through her brain right now. Her head was spinning; the alcohol muddled her thinking. She should have refused that third drink. She needed to get herself together.

"Gemma? What do you think?"

Gemma shook her head to get back to reality. "Sorry? I missed that."

"Do you think there's a way to fix this?"

"*No.*" It came out too harshly. She quickly softened her tone, seeing Anya's face fall. "No. He doesn't deserve you."

Anya looked down; her shoulders hunched further. "It was one mistake."

"Cheating on you? Multiple times? It doesn't sound like one mistake." She shook her head. Anya didn't look convinced. "Remember when we were sixteen and we talked about things that were unforgivable for us? You said—"

"I know what I said," Anya interrupted. For the first time tonight, she sounded close to tears. "But we were children then, Gem. We knew nothing about real relationships or the compromises they require sometimes."

Nausea swirled in Gemma's stomach and burned bitter in her throat. She took great care to put her glass down gently for fear she might smash it against the wall.

"No. I understand compromise, and this is not it. He doesn't deserve you."

"Doesn't he, though? He's a good man, Gemma. He loves me. We don't fight, he never ever yelled at me. We're *good* together. And he apologized. He admitted he made a mistake and apologized for it."

"He's been *cheating* on you. For weeks. Are you really ready to forget that and stay with him just because he's been slightly better than your father was?"

Anya's jaw dropped. By unspoken agreement, they'd never talked about those nights when she'd slept at Gemma's because her parents were "talking."

"That's not—" she stuttered.

"Isn't it? So you just love Ben so much that you would fight to stay with him, maybe marry him, even though you'd never trust him again?"

Anya looked away, her eyes overflowing. Gemma took her hand.

"Hey. I'm sorry. But you deserve *so* much better. You deserve someone who will love you and cherish you and who will always be honest with you. Someone who will tell you every day how amazing you are." Anya glanced at her, biting her lip, and Gemma continued, emboldened. "Someone who will watch sappy movies with you and take you out of town on summer nights to count the stars, and bring you cappuccino in bed on lazy Sunday mornings. Who will hold you every night and kiss you every morning, and know to bring you a hot water bottle and Hershey's kisses when the cramps hit—"

Anya let out a wet little chuckle. "I don't think any guy is going to be that good, Gem."

"Does it have to be a guy?"

She knew she'd said too much, dazed with the whiskey and emotions, careless as she'd never let herself be. Anya's eyes grew huge, confused.

"What?"

Gemma's heart tripped over itself as it sped to a gallop. "Okay, let's pretend I didn't say anything."

"No. What did you mean?" Anya's fingers tightened around her hand almost painfully.

"Anya…"

"Tell me. *Please.*"

Gemma had never been able to say no to her.

"I've loved you since we were fifteen," she whispered, her eyes on the half-empty glass, unable to look at her best friend in a moment that had every chance to break them. But if she was saying this, she was going to say it right. "I've loved you longer than that, truly, but I was fifteen when I realized that it wasn't only as a friend. And I've wanted to tell you so many times. That you're the loveliest girl in the whole world, inside and out; that you brighten my every day by just existing; that I think you're my soulmate. But… I was afraid, and I knew I would never be with you like that anyway." She sighed and bit her lip to keep her voice from trembling. "I just want you to be happy. So, so happy. Because you deserve all the best there is in the world, even if it's not with me."

When she dared to look up, Anya's eyes were wide, and the expression of distress on her beautiful face cut right through Gemma's heart. She *knew* it was a bad idea. She should have never said anything; she should have kept the truth in like a bird in a cage, the way she had all those years.

Gemma pushed away from the table; her chair screeched over the tiled floor. "I… I have to go. I have to… I'm sorry."

She didn't look back as she ran out of the bar.

8. CAPPUCCINO

THE KNOCK ON THE DOOR came on a Friday evening in late April.

Gemma was alone, buried in books as she studied for her first final the following week. Studying helped. It kept her busy and let her forget, if only for a while, how shattered she'd been since that disaster at the bar.

Six weeks. Six long, lonely weeks with no word from Anya. Even in her worst nightmares Gemma hadn't thought her coming out, if and when it finally happened, would end quite *that* badly. She'd dreaded awkwardness, distance, uncomfortable questions, but had been sure that in the end their friendship would survive. Clearly, she had been wrong.

But then—the knock on the door, and a shock of colors at eye level, roses and Peruvian lilies all mixed up and vivid, and Anya's sweet, earnest face peeking out from behind the flowers. Gemma's heart skipped a beat, stealing all breath from her lungs.

The bouquet was pushed into her arms, and she took it without thinking, stunned with the wave of emotions welling up in her chest. She'd always wondered what it would feel like to get flowers from someone—and then she would berate herself for falling back on stereotypes. She was a lesbian; surely it didn't work the same way between two women. Did it? Was there a textbook for these things?

Only now it wasn't even about the flowers, not really. Anya was here. Here was the chance Gemma had been too afraid to seek herself, right in front of her.

"I'm sorry," she let out in a rush. The words had been ready and waiting for weeks now. "I shouldn't have dumped my issues on you and definitely not in a moment like that. I was a terrible friend and I hope you can forgive me."

Anya shook her head. Her right eyebrow was raised in an incredulous arch.

"Do not even," she said. "This is my part, and I came prepared." She pointed to the bouquet in Gemma's arms. "Apology flowers." Then she reached out with a tall travel mug in her hand. "Post-apology coffee. The good kind."

"But—"

"But most importantly, unlike you, I actually have a reason to apologize. You trusted me with something precious and important, and I reacted like a caveman, and then disappeared without a word. It wasn't fair to you, and, even though I had my reasons, that's no excuse for hurting you. I'm so sorry."

She paused, biting her lip, and it struck Gemma how young and vulnerable she looked: more subdued than ever, with no make-up and her hair in a loose braid. Gemma ached to reach out, touch her in any of the hundred familiar ways they had for comfort, but before she could, Anya straightened up with the brave mask falling back into place.

"Is it okay if I come in?"

Gemma hadn't even realized they were still standing in the doorway. She moved out of the way and nearly tripped over the laundry basket in her hurry. "Of course. Sorry it's a mess. I've been busy and…" She shrugged.

Anya's smile was small and warm. "I don't mind. I've missed you, and there have been so many changes in the last few weeks.

I just want to talk to you. You've always been the one I talked to about important stuff."

A terrible thought shot through Gemma's head.

"Please tell me you haven't gotten engaged to Ben after all."

"What? No, of course not. Ben is history. You were right. He's not the sort of compromise I want."

"Oh. Okay, then. Let me just find a glass for the flowers and I'll be right with you."

A few minutes later, Gemma settled on her squeaky old desk chair and swiveled to face Anya, who was seated in her usual place on the bed. She handed Gemma the cup.

"One maple cappuccino with cinnamon on top, especially for you."

Gemma accepted the coffee, hoping that the trembling in her hands wasn't obvious. "Thank you. I didn't know they had maple cappuccino in Starbucks right now."

"They don't. It's from a different place. That's actually one of the changes I mentioned."

"You've changed your coffee provider? Impossible."

Anya laughed. "And yet, I did. In more ways than one." She took a deep breath. "I'm actually changing my job. I'll be joining them next month."

"What? But you love it at Starbucks!"

Anya shrugged; her fingers played with the corner of Gemma's blue comforter. "I do. But I've thought about moving on for a while now, about trying it somewhere smaller and more artisan. Bloody Coffee fits the bill."

"It's called *Bloody Coffee*? That sounds like a place catering to vampires. Or managed by vampires. Wait, are you sure they aren't out for your blood?" Gemma widened her eyes in exaggerated fright.

"Have you been binge watching *Vampire Diaries* again?" Anya chuckled. "No, I'm afraid they're as human as they come. But their coffee is amazing and they use all the different brewing methods and send their baristas to professional workshops all the time. And it just felt like the right moment. To start anew in all the ways." She paused with a smile. "I've moved out from my aunt's too."

Gemma could feel her jaw drop. "Really? That's huge!"

"Yeah. It's been nice to live rent-free, but I've had enough of the control and I can afford my own space now. Just a room in a student apartment, but it's mine, and nobody tells me what time to get home every day or stops me from having any visitors I want. Plus, it's only a five-minute walk from here." She chuckled. "Who knows, maybe I'll manage not to be late to classes for a change, now that I don't have to take the bus."

The look on Gemma's face must have been completely transparent because Anya frowned. "What? Do you think it was a bad idea?"

"No, it just feels weird. Such important changes in your life, and I wasn't there for any of them."

"I know. But… I needed this, you know? The time apart. To see who I am on my own and to process some stuff. I needed to make sure what I'm thinking and feeling is my own, and not affected by your presence." She reached over the short distance between the bed and chair to take Gemma's hand. "I know it was awfully selfish of me to disappear without a word and I hope you can forgive me for that. I knew that if I started speaking to you after our last conversation, I wouldn't be able to stop and then I would never know."

There was something in Anya's face, something soft and earnest, and Gemma found her voice shaky when she asked, "Know what?"

"If I'm really in love with you or just mirroring your affection."

Gemma tensed, jerking away from the cool touch of Anya's hand so hard her chair rode back and into the desk with a loud thump. "No. Please don't say things like this. You don't owe me anything just because I said I love you."

"Didn't you mean it?"

"Of course I meant it. I meant everything I said. But that doesn't mean you have to reciprocate. I don't expect you to change for me. We can just be friends like we always were. I can keep this to myself. It won't get weird, I promise, just…" She dropped her head in her hands; her heart beat in a panicked staccato. "Don't lie for my sake. Not to me, not to yourself."

Anya's voice was soft and careful. "That's the thing though. I'm not lying. I've loved you since I met you too. Always. You've been my *best friend*. Do you know how many times I've imagined spending our whole lives together and how perfect that would be? I just never thought it could mean romantically." She huffed, and Gemma looked up to see her amused face. "And it's so stupid, because I've always considered myself an LGBT ally, but somehow it didn't click that I, personally, could ever be attracted to anyone but boys. Like, being gay is all good in an abstract way, but a girl needs a husband and children, and that's that. All my life, I haven't once considered I could be a lesbian."

"Because you're *not*."

"No. But I am bi."

Gemma felt as though she could cry. "Anya. You just… I'm afraid that you may just be letting the situation sway you in a direction you'd never have taken otherwise. You're fresh out of a long-term relationship. I came out to you by declaring my undying love for you. I think it may be a little… confusing."

"I'm not confused. I might have been at first, with the break-up and how many feelings your confession brought up in me, but then I decided to approach it methodically."

"Methodically," Gemma echoed weakly.

Anya grinned, infuriatingly beautiful even as she shook the ground beneath Gemma's feet. "Yes, like they taught us in science class, remember? I needed to test my hypothesis and I needed to do it in a controlled environment, hence the distance from you. I designed a few experiments and set the time period to measure my responses. I would say the process has been immensely educational."

Gemma shook her head, amused despite the nerves. "What did you do?"

"I went to a few meetings of the gay-straight alliance on campus and talked to people. Explored the gay club in town. Kissed a few girls."

Gemma gasped. "You did what?!"

Anya bit her lip. "I know. A bit iffy when the goal was to prove or disprove I was in love with *you*, specifically. But I needed to check my reactions to actual physical contact, not just to my thoughts and fantasies, and I couldn't approach you without being certain. And I am, now. Girls are really, really appealing to me. Sexy. Amazing. Got me thinking about all kinds of things I would love to do with them."

"Oh, my god, please stop." Gemma covered her eyes. She was sure her cheeks must be deep red by now. Anya continued, undeterred.

"But I haven't done anything more than a kiss with any of them. Because they were not you, and I'd rather do these things with you. I want to do everything with you, to be everything for you." Anya moved to kneel in front of Gemma's chair, her eyes intense. "So no, don't tell me I am confused. This is not a phase, or a rebound thing. I want to be with you. If you still want me."

A small move forward, a squeak of the chair, and then Anya's lips were on hers, softer and sweeter than anything Gemma ever dared to imagine. When she pulled back, Gemma's head was spinning. Anya looked a little stunned too; her fingers flew up to her mouth.

"Oh." She licked her lips; a smile started in the corners of her mouth and spread to her whole face until her eyes were dancing. "Is that a yes?"

"*Yes.*"

The coffee went cold. Gemma didn't care.

9. INSTANT

THERE WAS NO PROPER COFFEE in Gemma's room, just the half-decent instant she always bought, and she briefly considered running out for the good stuff, but one look at Anya's lovely face on her pillow was enough to banish the idea. She wouldn't risk missing the chance to see her wake up after their first night together—*together*—with that sleepy smile of hers and her bare arms stretching up, maybe the blankets riding down a little…

Blushing, Gemma stopped that train of thought. They'd only been together for a few weeks, and it had been a time of slow exploration in stolen hours between paper writing and reviewing and exams, a time of discovering how much had changed for them with this new kind of relationship and how much remained the same as it always had been. But now finals were officially over, and Anya had stayed at Gemma's overnight for the first time since *that* talk.

Gemma's body still hummed with the memory.

The electric kettle clicked off; water bubbled happily inside. She took out the milk and poured water over the prepared powder. The mere act of making *two* cups of coffee this morning filled her with heady joy. But there were nerves too. Last night was like a dream capping off a period of unreal, sleep-deprived happiness. The school year was over, and they hadn't discussed what would happen now. Were they going to let people know they were together? Here? Back at home? Were they *official*?

At the smell of coffee, Anya stirred, turned onto her back, and hummed softly. The covers slid down, revealing the gentle slope of her breasts, and Gemma's breath stopped. The view was even more gorgeous in the morning sunlight falling through the window.

Anya opened her eyes and stretched luxuriously; her fingers slid down over one brown nipple to rest on her stomach. "Mm, coffee?" she asked hopefully, her eyes bright and happy, full of joy.

Gemma swallowed through her dry throat and picked up a cup. "I only have instant."

"Mm, that's okay. We'll go for proper lattes later. I have to show my girlfriend off at my new coffeeshop, after all. Not to mention, take her out on a date."

"You do?"

Anya grinned. "Of course. But that's for later. *Much* later. Coffee first, and then I want you back in this bed. I'm going to rock your world, miss."

Gemma laughed, her heart expanding with happiness. "You already did."

ABOUT KATE FIERRO: Kate Fierro spent ten years translating, editing and reviewing other people's words before making an impulse decision to write down some of her own. She hasn't been able to stop ever since. Kate lives in Europe and is bilingual, with more love for her adopted language than her native one. Her debut novel, *Love Starved*, was published by Interlude Press in 2015.

GILDED SCALES

by Julia Ember

THE BOYS FORMED A LINE in front of the aeldorman's throne. Today, they would receive the golden armbands that marked them as warriors. Two attendants wove in and out of the line, sprinkling them with dried goat's blood and iron filings. The boys stood shirtless, skin pimpled with cold. On their bare chests they had painted the symbols of their patron gods in vivid blue dye. A circle for Hursa, goddess of horses and the earth. A jagged wave for Brim, lord of the oceans. A shield for the warrior god Cempa, slayer of monsters. A cross, for the new Christian god some in the village had adopted.

Fenn glowered as her brother, who had never so much as swung an axe and was more likely to slay a giant with his terrible singing than with a sword, waited to be called forward. Anselm glanced over his shoulder at her and smirked, his expression rubbing salt into her already wounded pride. Under the table, Fenn wove her fingers together and fluttered her hands like wings, a rude gesture that evoked the winged god, Flfer, and his cowardice. Fenn knew that Anselm had noticed, because even in the dim candlelight of the Mead Hall, she saw his cheeks flush.

Beside her on the long bench, Ma shook her head and pinched Fenn's thigh.

Aeldorman Wulfgar called the first boy. Cedric had broad shoulders, arms roped with muscle, and a roguish smile that had once made Fenn's stomach squirm. He shot a bow with so much precision even Pa called him skilled, though Fenn's footwork with a blade was much better.

He stepped forward to the throne and took a knee. Wulfgar rested his hand on Cedric's honey-colored curls. The aeldorman wore a jeweled ring on each of his bony fingers, and so many bracelets circled his slender arms that he appeared to wear gauntlets of gold.

"Will you pledge to serve me faithfully?" the aeldorman asked.

Cedric mumbled his response. Fenn scoffed into her mug of mead. How hard was it to say yes with some conviction? If she had been up there, her voice would have projected so the entire hall could hear.

Ma leaned over and pressed her lips to Fenn's ear. "Try to be happy for him. This is a big day for Cedric and for your brother."

Fenn crossed her arms and looked pointedly away from Ma. She had pled her case before Aeldorman Wulfgar a hundred times, asking him to let her make the oath and become a warrior. And each time, he had said the same thing: *Warrior maidens are just myths. You're a pretty girl, Fenn. Go home and find a husband.*

She knew that he meant Cedric. The whole village, including her family and Cedric himself, all expected it.

The aeldorman held out the armband. It was expertly crafted with three distinct ropes of gold, twisted together to form a braid and an enormous cerulean-blue gemstone at its center. Such a gift was a mark of the aeldorman's high esteem for Cedric.

Cedric dipped his head as he accepted his band so his shaggy blonde hair fell into his face. He tried to push it back, but a lock stuck to his lips. Fenn had kissed him once. Their teeth had bumped together. And Cedric had sort of engulfed her mouth; his upper lip brushed the tip of her nose. When they'd pulled apart, he'd left a trail of moisture behind that had felt more like snot than romance.

It wasn't fair that he got to become a warrior and earn glory in the eyes of the gods when she could not. The injustice of it made Fenn feel like screaming and storming out of the hall. But when Cedric turned to face the rest of the hall, his eyes sought out Fenn's for her approval, and she softened just a little.

The aeldorman worked his way through the line of boys. He called each of them in turn and prompted them to swear the oath. Then he offered them a tapered golden armband. None were as grand as the band he had given Cedric, but they were still the most valuable things most of the boys would ever own.

When it was Anselm's turn, he gave Fenn another sly smile before he took a knee. She wanted to hurl her mug at the back of her brother's head. She doubted he'd be quick enough to duck.

To Fenn's further irritation, Anselm didn't stumble as he spoke the words of his oath. His voice rang out true and clear, and, when he rose, everyone in the room applauded. His armband was a little too big and it slipped down his bicep to cradle in his elbow. But by all the laws of the kingdom, he was a recognized as a warrior now, no longer child. He could vote in the council and own a farm freehold. He could take a spouse and raise a family.

He could be called to war at any time.

Without an armband, Fenn couldn't fight or own property or even decide whom she would marry. Her father would give her to a husband, and then she would be his, whether that was what she wanted or not. Such were the laws in Lindeshelm, in all of Ebrauc. And it had always struck Fenn as ironic that, in order to be truly free, she needed a band of a metal that looked like a chain.

Ma scooted down the bench to make room, and Anselm wedged himself next to Fenn. Something hot burned in her chest. She couldn't tell if it was pride or anger or a bit of both.

Her brother picked up his mug and took a long drink. His chin trembled ever so slightly, and his eyes glistened with restrained tears. His breathing was shallow and rapid. He had put on a show for his friends, but Fenn was reminded that this was not what Anselm wanted either. Against their father's wishes and Fenn's understanding, her brother had converted to the new faith. He wanted to travel to the monastery on the coast, to pray and meditate and learn to read. She wrapped her arm around his back and gave him a squeeze.

As the last boy received his armband, the doors to the hall flew open. Shocked, everyone turned to face the entrance. The relationship between an aeldorman and his fighters was a special, sacred thing in the eyes of the gods. There were warriors stationed at the doors to make sure that the solemnity and sanctity of the ceremony were preserved. No one was allowed to enter or leave once it had started.

A tall, lean warrior marched into the hall. His blond hair was so soaked with blood it appeared almost red. He bore an angry cut across his left cheek. The fabric of his tunic had been burned away, and the exposed skin of his shoulder was blistered and raw. There was a cross on his shield, bordered in gold. His wide eyes scanned the room.

The guards rushed in behind him. All around the hall, the other warriors rose to their feet, ceremony forgotten. Fenn perched on the edge of the bench and wondered if she should draw her dagger. Ma had warned her not to bring it, and she would be in trouble if her parents saw, but she knew she could throw it true—right into the white of the stranger's eye.

Only Aeldorman Wulfgar remained seated. He studied the man's face as he approached the throne. With a tired sigh, the stranger sank to one knee.

"Ecberth?" the aeldorman asked. "Why are you here? Everyone, pleased be seated."

The aeldorman's recognition of the stranger quieted the hall, despite the man's rough appearance. Wulfgar indicated to a servant standing by the wall, and the girl rushed to bring a stool.

"I have come from the sacred field," Ecberth said and eased onto the stool with a stiffness that made Fenn wonder if his leg was also injured. "Two days ago, my village of Yric was destroyed. We woke to smoke and flames, and a great winged shadow that covered the sun. The dragon attacked us and thereafter made its home in the mounds of the sacred field among the dead and their gold.

"We went after it," Ecberth continued. He took a deep breath and motioned the serving girl for a mug of mead. After a sip, he gasped, "We confronted the beast in Cyng Aella's mound. I am the only one of my party to survive. But inside the tomb, we heard a girl as well as the beast. She was crying. No doubt the beast has captured her. It may at this moment be subjecting her to all manner of foul things. My liege, Aeldorman Hfrostan, requests that you assist us in putting the beast down before it razes another village."

The Mead Hall erupted in hushed whispers. Fenn exchanged a glance with Cedric.

For twenty years, there had been peace in Lindeshelm. New warriors had no real reason or opportunity to prove themselves, and so they were given the armbands by the aeldorman's decision.

Since Ma had been a child, the town had not been raided by the Northmen who came from across the narrow sea. The local aeldormen had kept faith with one another and the king. The low creatures that used to live in the crevices of the mountains, snatching children and sheep, had not resurfaced.

Whoever defeated the dragon would earn glory and respect throughout the whole kingdom. If she fought a dragon and lived, Aeldorman Wulfgar would have no choice but to recognize Fenn's skills, to give her the armband she coveted in front of everyone in the Mead Hall. There would be no more pressure to marry Cedric. They could fight beside each other as equals.

"I will not force my warriors to undertake this." Aeldorman Wulfgar slouched on his throne and ran a hand through his graying brown hair. "But those who wish to volunteer may go with my blessing."

This struck Fenn as cowardly. The sacred field was a two-day ride from Lindeshelm. But what was that distance to a dragon? It could fly straight over the mountains. If they didn't act, they could be its next victims. And what of the unfortunate girl? Would the aeldorman just leave her to be tortured, eaten?

Ecberth glanced around the room. A few hands shot up, including those of Cedric and some of his more eager friends. They rose from their places on the bench and, nodding to the aeldorman, assembled by the door. Anselm sat as still as stone beside Fenn.

"If we leave it alone, it may do nothing," Osryth, the aeldorman's second wife, commented. She walked up to her husband's throne and stood behind him. Her fine blue gown hung all the way to the floor and rustled when she moved. "Dragons are attracted to gold, are they not? And they are known to sometimes sleep for a hundred years once they have found a suitable lair. It can guard Cyng Aella's tomb from thieves."

Wulfgar took Osryth's hand but inclined his head to the boys who stood ready by the door. "Here are some of our fine young warriors to aid you, Ecberth. For now, we will keep the rest of our fighters close at hand. Should the dragon venture farther afield, we do not want to be left undefended ourselves."

Ecberth frowned but bowed his head. In Ebrauc, the word of an aeldorman could only be contradicted by the king himself. Ecberth could not push his case further.

"I'll go," Fenn said, scrambling up from her bench. Her wool dress caught on a knot of wood, but she managed to get to her feet without tripping. She pulled her dagger from its sheath. The blade glittered in the light of the shrunken tallow candles. She had sharpened it to precision and she saw the flicker of surprise and appraisal in Ecberth's eyes as she lifted it. Aeldorman Wulfgar would never give her the chance to prove herself, but maybe this stranger would be different.

The hall went silent. The aeldorman shook his head. Anselm spluttered something hollow about girls and fights of a lifetime, though he knew nothing about either and hadn't volunteered himself. Ma's hand flew to her mouth. Pa's jaw clenched with anger. But nobody laughed outright, and Fenn thanked the gods for that.

"You?" Cedric finally demanded. He folded his arms over his broad chest. "Fenn, you cannot. I forbid it."

From him, of all people, the words were like a slap. Fenn lifted her chin.

"I mean that it is my job to keep you safe," he stammered. "I won't fail you."

"I am inclined to agree," Aeldorman Wulfgar said. "The beast has already taken one girl as prisoner."

"If the dragon has an affinity for young girls, then perhaps he will not kill me after he incinerates the rest of you," Fenn snapped.

Ma pinched her again.

Ecberth coughed loudly into his fist. Fenn thought that he was laughing, which made her angrier still. His dark eyes danced, and little wrinkles appeared around them when he said, "My shield brother waits outside for us. The young warriors can leave with him as soon as they are equipped. The girl can ride with me in the morning. I'll keep her as safe as I can."

Fenn closed her eyes and prayed to all the gods at once that Wulfgar would not deny her this.

The aeldorman's brow creased as he studied her. Fenn stared back at him as fiercely as she could without being openly insolent.

Finally, Wulfgar sighed. "Go, Fenn, but whatever happens to you, do not blame anyone but yourself."

*   *   *

FENN BARELY SLEPT THAT NIGHT. She stole a pair of Anselm's breeches and dressed for the next day's ride, then sat by her window. She looked up at the stars twinkling behind a curtain of sheer gray fog. She imagined a great shadow passing in front of them. She imagined a beast made of black smoke, twisting up to the sky. She imagined a scaled monster the size of a ship, purring like a cat and curling around Cedric's prone body. She imagined a well of flame, bubbling in the depths of Cyng Aella's tomb, engulfing her.

But when she finally crawled into her bed and closed her eyes, she dreamed of glory.

She woke before everyone else and gathered what supplies she could: her father's old sword, slightly rusted, dried lamb and cheese, a skin of water. Then she snuck out into the crisp morning. If this was goodbye and she would never see her family again, she didn't know what to say, so it was better that she left before Ma could try again to change her mind.

Anselm hadn't spoken to her since before the ceremony in the Mead hall. Fenn had tried, but she could tell he was humiliated that Fenn had volunteered when he would not. But he couldn't fight, and Fenn was happy for him to stay home, abed and embarrassed, rather than disgrace himself and their family on the sacred fields.

Ecberth waited for her outside the aeldorman's hall. His dun horse was already saddled, and he looked cleaner than the night before, though no less tired. His hair was golden blond once more, and someone had scrubbed his bronze shield to a shine. But his eyes were bloodshot, with dark purple circles beneath them. He reclined against the wall of the Mead Hall, chewing a strand of wheat speckled with dark ergot.

The seers sometimes ate the fungus to commune with the gods more easily, but Ecberth wore the cross of the Christian god. Last night, imagining what the dragon might look like had excited Fenn more than scared her. But perhaps Ecberth chewed the ergot to twist the reality of the creature in his memories, to make it seem less monstrous.

She swallowed and gripped her pack more tightly.

"Last chance, Fenn, daughter of Aswald," Ecberth called out. "I can ride without you, and you can go back to bed."

Fenn glanced up at the sky, at the rays of gold cutting through the purple dawn. Ma would wake any minute to milk the goats and knead the dough she would bake into bread. If Fenn lost her nerve now, that was her future too.

"Too late for that," she said and tied her pack to the horse's saddle.

*   *   *

ECBERTH DID NOT MAKE A good travelling companion. More than once, Fenn tried to engage him in conversation about his past or about the beast they were to face. But despite the humor she'd seen in his eyes in the Mead Hall, he kept most of his answers short. Perhaps he thought it best not to become too attached to her, since she would probably die.

In any case, she had learned that he had not actually seen the dragon. He had survived because he had been ordered to guard the entrance of the tomb. After hearing his companions scream, he had tried to run inside and had been met with a wall of fire and molten gold. The blood in his hair and on his shield had been his own, from a deep wound in his scalp caused by a beam in the tomb falling on him as he fled. He had known it was too late to save his companions, but, from within, he had heard the maiden whimpering.

"Perhaps the dragon will speak to us and tell us what it wants," Fenn said on the morning of the second day, as they climbed the final mountain that overlooked the sacred field. They walked beside the tired mare, and her feet ached. "If it thinks you might exchange me."

Ecberth scoffed. "I don't think the beast is so clever. And besides, if we exchanged you, your fate would be sealed. I thought you wanted to fight."

"I might escape," Fenn muttered. "After it's gone to sleep. I might kill it."

"Or you might not," Ecberth said and rolled his eyes. "And if you didn't, we'd be in the same situation as now: a dragon occupying Cyng Aella's mound and a girl trapped inside."

"My village wouldn't send anyone to rescue me," Fenn snapped, even as her heart clenched. By now, Cedric was probably dead, and her brother would never risk himself to save her. Pa might not even have noticed she was missing. Whoever this girl was, Fenn hoped she was worth more to her village than Fenn was worth to her own.

At least, if she risked herself, she knew it was her own choice.

Ecberth shook his head. "You are a fighter in my war band. Honor would demand that I raise a party and go in after you, if I believed you still lived."

Fenn's cheeks stretched with a smile. Ecberth had called her a fighter. Not a maiden, not a nuisance, but a *fighter*. "The dragon and I might get along quite well."

Ecberth made a disgusted grunt at the back of his throat.

They reached the top of the mountain and sat to catch their breaths. Ecberth offered Fenn the last of their dried lamb, and she tore into it gratefully. She was not used to the pace they'd kept, and her appetite was sharp. If the dragon took her, it might be a long time before she saw food again.

Below them, the sacred field stretched to the sea on the horizon. Burial mounds rose out of the earth, some as tall as oaks, others the height of Fenn's waist. Cyng Aella's mound was near the center, in the circle of kings. Despite the height of the mountain, Fenn could see a ring of bodies scattered around the entrance to Aella's tomb. The warriors' armor caught the sun and glimmered.

She shielded her eyes and squinted, searching for Cedric. But the corpses were so splayed and bloody, it was impossible to identify any of the men at a distance. Even as bile burned in her throat, she nursed the hope that he was alive.

It took them the better part of the day to pick their way down the mountain's rocky face. And once they reached the field, they moved even more slowly, keeping under the cover of bushes and trees, lest the dragon appear in the sky and see them. They left the mare and their gear outside the mound of Cyng Wullha. The horse pranced nervously when Fenn tied her to a scraggly tree, but she seemed relieved to be left behind. When Fenn patted her neck, she settled enough to start grazing.

The field was eerily quiet. Fenn couldn't hear any birds or even the rustle of the wind. And if the dead had anything to say, they were keeping it to themselves for now.

As they walked closer, Ecberth's skin grew clammy with sweat. His cheeks paled, and his steps began to tremble. Pity made Fenn's chest constrict. She did not dare ask how many people his village had lost or if he was expecting to find a dead friend at the tomb, so she reached out and clasped his shoulder instead. He took a deep breath, and his steps grew steadier.

At the entrance to the tomb, Ecberth crouched low and checked the pulse of one of the corpses—a mere boy with a patchy beard and milky blue eyes. When Ecberth pulled away, his jaw was clenched. Fenn wanted to ask him who the boy was, but she sensed it would be like ripping a scab off a newly closed wound.

"We won't go in," Ecberth said. "Entering and seeking out the dragon has led everyone to death so far. But if we hide here, we might be able to surprise it when it emerges to feed. We can shelter in one of the smaller mounds at night and watch in the day."

Fenn thought that the creature had probably eaten more than enough already, given the number of men who had gone into the tomb, but she bit her tongue. Many of the men were Ecberth's friends. And as angry as she was with Cedric for leaving her behind, she did not want to imagine a dragon picking its teeth with his bones.

From the depths of the mound, someone let out a thin, high-pitched cry. Ecberth pressed his fingers to his lips and tugged Fenn behind a tree. They listened. The cries grew louder. They were not screams of pain or fear, but something lonelier and more desperate. The cry gripped Fenn and twisted her.

"This girl—did she come from your village?" she whispered.

"No," Ecberth said. "The dragon killed a few people when it burned our town, but no one is missing."

"Do you know how long it was hiding here? Before it attacked you?"

Only lords and kings, aeldormen and fabled warriors were buried in the sacred field. Everyone else lived and died within the radius of their towns and were buried or burned according to the customs of the gods their family served. It had been years since a new mound had been built in the field. How long had this girl been alone in the dark with only a dead king and a monster for company? Maybe she had come with a band of warriors, intent on fighting the beast. Maybe she, too, had been told that whatever her fate, it was her own fault.

And maybe Fenn could not kill the dragon, but she was lighter than the other warriors and she carried no cumbersome shield. She had hunted deer in the woods around the town for years. She could move softly.

She sprinted forward into the mouth of the tomb. Too late, Ecberth tried to grab for her arm. He hissed after her, but Fenn ignored him.

Inside, the air of the tomb was surprisingly cold, though smoke lingered, so thick it was hard for Fenn to breathe. More bodies lined the tomb's narrow entrance. She stopped and listened to make sure that Ecberth had not followed her. She didn't want to be responsible for his death, as foolishly as she had invited her own.

She crept forward, searching for Cedric among the bodies, but the corpses were burned beyond any hope of recognition. Fenn noticed that their golden armbands had been stripped off, some violently enough to dislocate shoulders.

She removed her boots and tiptoed. As her bare feet brushed charred and bloated flesh, she had to bite on her hand to keep from screaming. She pressed herself as tightly as she could to the walls and prayed to Cempa that the shadows would hide her. Now that her initial rush of pity and energy had faded, her heart drummed with fear.

All of the kings' tombs had the same basic layout: an entrance hall, a central chamber for the king's treasures, and a cramped burial nook made of stone at the very back. Fenn followed the winding entrance as it carved its way deeper into the mound. The crying had stopped, so perhaps the girl and the monster were asleep.

When she reached the central chamber, Fenn was so awestruck that she forgot her fear. The entire cavern was filled with gold. Goblets, armbands, crowns, and coins without number formed hills that sloped up the stone walls. It was enough treasure to fill a dozen ships or more. Cyng Aella had been powerful and rich, but no kingdom would bury so much. The dragon had been building its hoard, creating a nest of gold.

Fenn shuddered. It probably intended to raise a brood of monsters right at the heart of their sacred field. She gripped her rusted sword so tightly her fingers tingled.

She couldn't see the dragon anywhere. She breathed a sigh of relief. The creature must have already left to feed or to gather more plunder from another helpless village. She felt a stab of guilt, thinking about Ecberth. If he was still near the mouth of the tomb, he would face the dragon alone if it returned. The beast might now be feasting on Ecberth's mare and all their supplies. Fenn needed to get the girl, and then they all needed to hide.

Breathing hard, she scanned the mountains of gold for the girl. She located her in the far corner, near the corridor that led to Cyng Aella's burial chamber. The girl slept on her side with her knees curled to her chest. She wore a torn and dirty gown made from rough blue wool. Her hair was a mess of tangled red curls. A flickering torch stood in a gold vase behind her.

Fenn rushed toward her, moving faster and more confidently now that she could see the dragon was not waiting to devour her.

"Hello?" she called into the gloom. "Quick, wake up! We have to get you out of here before it comes back."

The girl shifted and rolled over. Fenn extended her free hand toward her, as she would to a frightened horse. The girl blinked at her. She had wide, clear blue eyes framed by a multitude of long, black lashes. Her skin was alabaster white and smooth as fresh cream. She was round and lavish, with a full belly and gentle curves.

Fenn swallowed hard. It was no wonder the dragon had kept her. Despite her tattered clothing, the girl was undoubtedly the most beautiful person Fenn had ever seen. She looked like one of the angels the Christians painted in the new church they had built at the edge of her village. The dragon would never have accepted Fenn, with her limp blonde hair and sallow complexion, as a substitute.

The girl stared at Fenn with her hypnotic eyes. Her rosebud lips curled into a faint smile and she sat up. Fenn took another step toward her. But then she noticed how the light around the girl had shifted. The torch illuminated a shadow on the wall behind her.

The shadow was as large as a barn, with folded wings and great horns that stretched to the ceiling.

Fenn's instincts screamed at her to turn around, to face the beast that had crept up behind her and meet her gods as a warrior. But she hesitated, and the girl raised her hands. Her fingers were tipped in fire as yellow as molten gold. A demon, hidden in the form of this beautiful girl.

Fenn could picture how so many warriors had spent their last seconds: turning to face the dragon that wasn't there, exposing their backs to the monster with an angel's eyes. If she turned around, she was sure she would die.

Hands shaking with fear, Fenn dropped her sword and backed away, deeper into the tomb.

*   *   *

In a few strides, Fenn reached the back of the tomb. She searched frantically for somewhere to hide, but Cyng Aella's burial chamber was hardly wide enough for her to squeeze around his coffin. She felt along the back of the damp wall for any loose stones or hidden exits, but there was nothing.

She remembered what Ecberth had told her, about the wall of fire he'd met when he tried to save his friends. If she remained in the open, the dragon girl would incinerate her where she stood. She swallowed down a wave of nausea and moved to Cyng Aella's stone coffin.

The lid was so heavy and firmly sealed by time that Fenn had to brace her legs against the wall and push with her back to shift it. When she peered over the edge into the coffin, she expected to stare into the hollowed eye sockets of the dead king. Instead, she found a flight of narrow slate stone steps that led down into the dark.

Fenn didn't hesitate. She swung her legs over the edge of the coffin and dropped onto the first step. She pulled the lid back as far as she could, but, from her angle, it was impossible for her to fully seal the coffin. A narrow strip of light illuminated the steps around her.

Fenn descended, taking the stairs two and three at a time. The stone was cold and slick under her bare feet. She had no idea where the passage might lead. The bards who visited the Mead Hall at Lindeshelm, who told stories of the kings and the sacred field, had never described a hidden stairwell like this.

She wondered if the builders had created a secret entrance because they planned to rob the tomb after Cyng Aella was laid to rest. It was a violation of the gods, and those who stole from the burial mounds could never enter the great hall of Heofonsetl to feast for eternity. But not everyone shared those beliefs anymore and robberies had become more common in the past few years. She prayed that Cwaltt, the hag goddess who nurtured the dead, would not hold a grudge against her for opening the king's coffin.

At the bottom of the stairs, she found herself in a large room with a carved, vaulted stone ceiling. It was ornately furnished with rich carpets, unfaded despite the passage of a hundred years, chairs carved from red oak, an assortment of golden dishes and jewels. On a low bed in the corner, Cyng Aella slept. His body had wilted with time, and what remained was a mess of exposed brown bone and saggy, leathered skin. A few locks of gray hair still clung to the skull.

Fenn sank down against the wall opposite the dead king. She was still trapped, but at least for now she had a stone floor to separate her from the fire-breathing creature above. If the dragon did not follow her, she could wait here for hours, days if need be, and then try to sneak past the beast again. It had not heard her until she called out. If she could wait until it fell asleep again, she might escape to safety.

But if she waited too long, Ecberth might come back with more men, as he had promised. Then their deaths would be on her hands. She cursed herself for her foolishness. Why had she rushed into the cave? Why had she believed she could do what so many men could not? They had been seasoned warriors, and she was just a silly girl with too many dreams.

Ecberth had seen something in her, and it had been enough to make him contradict the word of her aeldorman. She had failed him. She could have waited and earned glory alongside Ecberth as the dragon emerged. Now, she was probably going to die here, alone, under the earth.

She wasn't even sure that anyone would mourn her. Pa might rejoice that he had escaped the predicament of a difficult daughter who wouldn't marry and settle. Anselm would finally be free of her shadow, never to be compared to her again.

Cedric would take a wife who would be meek, gentle, and never embarrass him in front of everyone in the Mead Hall.

Ma might miss her a little.

Fenn curled her knees up to her chest, buried her face, and began to cry.

*   *   *

FENN WAITED IN THE DIM chamber for what seemed like hours. Unable to see the sun, she passed the time by whispering stories to Cyng Aella's corpse. She was thirsty; exhaustion made her bones ache and her eyelids droop.

The sweet smells of roasting meat and dripping fat wafted down the stairs into the chamber, cutting through the musty scents of decay and wet earth. Despite her hunger, it made Fenn feel sick. The dragon girl was probably roasting one of her victims. She imagined a charred human corpse slowly turning on a spit.

Then she heard soft footsteps padding across the floor of the chamber above. She froze. The low grind of moving stone sent shivers coursing down her back. The smell of meat grew stronger, and Fenn's stomach roiled. She felt around for her sword, before remembering that she had dropped it in her retreat from the beast. Cyng Aella's corpse held no sword or axe. He had been a peaceful king, a ruler who presided over a time of trade and plenty, and his burial reflected that life.

Fenn shut her eyes and pleaded again with Cwaltt not to curse her. If the temperamental goddess looked unfavorably on what she was about to do, Fenn would be condemned to wander the earth as a shade for all time. She crawled across the floor to Cyng Aella's body. Grimacing, she ripped the king's brittle shin bone from his knee socket. The sound of cracking bone echoed in the chamber.

The footsteps drew nearer, careful and slow. Tears of fear welled in Fenn's eyes.

"Stay back!" she shouted. "I have a crossbow."

Her voice trembled with the lie. It was the most dangerous weapon she could think of, and yet, what was a crossbow to a dragon? Even if she had one, she didn't know how to fire it. The bolt would probably miss altogether or graze the creature's hide. That would make it angrier.

"Don't turn your back on me," a soft voice called. "Please."

Fenn positioned herself in the corner of the chamber with her back to the wall. She sank into a fighting crouch the way she had practiced with Cedric and raised the bone. It had splintered with a jagged edge, and she hoped that made it look more intimidating. Her knees shook, and her chest was so tight she couldn't breathe.

The dragon girl appeared in the doorway. Her bright blue eyes surveyed the room. Her gaze flickered from the king's body to Fenn's face. She clutched a golden plate, laden with what appeared to be a chicken thigh and an assortment of berries. In the dim light, her alabaster skin had an emerald green hue that reminded Fenn of scales. From her biceps down to her slender wrists, she wore a collection of golden armbands. Some were plain and unadorned; others were accented with twists and stones; some snug enough to fit her, others were so large they jingled as she moved.

Fenn jabbed the bone in the monster's direction. She was not going to be swayed so easily. Who knew what game the beast was playing? The dragon girl could be trying to lure Fenn into the chamber above. Perhaps she could not breathe fire in her human form and needed more space to transform into the winged creature Fenn had seen in her shadow.

The girl gracefully folded her legs beneath her and sat in the doorway. She rested the plate on her knee and popped a strawberry into her mouth. A line of red juice dribbled down her chin. Fenn stared, and her grip on the bone slackened.

"I'm Bryne," the monster chirped. She pushed the plate across the floor to Fenn. A few of the berries rolled off the plate and under Cyng Aella's bed.

Fenn scrambled out of the way, half-expecting the plate to burst into flames.

"Don't," the creature—Bryne—ground out in a gravelly voice that reminded Fenn of a crackling fire, "turn your back to me."

For a heartbeat, Fenn was tempted to do exactly that. If she went to her end bravely, the warrior god Cempa might put in a word for her with the hag that would cancel out her defiling of Cyng Aella's body and tomb. She could throw the bone like a dagger, then turn around, squeeze her eyes shut and wait for the flames to engulf her. In such a small space, so close to the monster, it might not take very long. It might be over before she could process the pain of it.

The girl held up a steady hand, and Fenn saw real fear in her eyes. A long, winged shadow extended up the stairs behind her. "Please."

"Why?" Fenn demanded. Her voice trembled with the question, and she was ashamed. She widened her fighting stance but did not throw the bone.

Bryne exhaled sharply, and a small puff of smoke curled from her lips. "Because if you do, I'll transform. And I won't be able to stop myself from killing you."

*   *   *

THE BONE SLID FROM FENN'S hand. When she had first seen Bryne's shadow, all her fighter's training had told her to turn, to face the monster head on, rather than let it devour her from behind. Had she not noticed the slight flicker of the flames dancing in Bryne's hands, Fenn would have turned to fight, and she'd have died. She had done nothing, not yet, that was worthy of resurrection in the halls of Heofonsetl. If she had died, it would have been final.

Fenn sank to the floor. Without taking her eyes off the girl, she pulled the plate of food toward herself with her bare toe.

"I found your boots," Bryne said, as if the status of her footwear was Fenn's greatest concern. "I left them at the top of the stairs. If you want them, I can get them."

Fenn nodded, but only to see if the dragon girl would really leave at her request. Bryne's graceful, timid movements reminded her of their family's barn cat. Fenn had watched him hunt on many occasions. He would lie down in a patch of sun, stretched and relaxed, eyes blinking slowly, while the mouse he was stalking got comfortable. Then, as the little rodent lifted a morsel of grain to its chubby cheeks, the cat would strike in a fury of orange fur and claws.

Fenn was not going to be the mouse. She would remain wary.

Bryne rose and trotted back up the stairs.

As soon as the other girl was out of sight, Fenn seized a handful of the berries and stuffed them into her mouth. They were juicy, sweet and cool, and they soothed some of the dryness in her throat. She lifted the chicken next and sniffed it, just to be sure it smelled familiar.

A few moments later, Bryne returned with Fenn's brown leather boots. She moved so silently that Fenn hadn't even heard her descending the stairs again. The thought alarmed her.

Bryne made to cross the room, holding the boots out in front of her. But as the girl stepped over the threshold of the door, Fenn dove for the bone again. Bryne sighed and sank into a kneeling position by the door.

The dragon girl, her expression serene and patient, watched Fenn eat. She positioned the boots beside Cyng Aella's bed and began braiding her auburn hair, utterly unconcerned by Fenn or her shinbone weapon. And although Fenn knew she should stay vigilant, should stay afraid, she found herself calming too.

When Fenn had eaten most of the berries and stripped the chicken thigh down to the bone, Bryne spoke. "You're the first to see me for what I am."

"A monster?" Fenn gave a mocking laugh. "How fortunate for me."

Bryne scowled. "That is certainly what most of them came looking for."

Fenn nodded. She, too, had come looking for a monster and, now that she had seen the reality of what Bryne was, she still wasn't entirely sure what she'd found. Certainly, Bryne was powerful, but she also wasn't the great, devilish creature that Fenn had been expecting. If Ecberth came crashing in now and slew Bryne where she sat, Fenn wasn't sure how she would feel.

"What did they do? The men, when they saw you?" Fenn asked, her tone gentler.

"They would storm in and hiss or shout, 'Girl, where is the beast?' And I would reply, 'The beast?'"

A faint smile tugged at Byrne lips. Then she tilted her head, and mimicked an angry, deep voice. "That foul creature! The dragon who haunts these sacred mounds!' I would reply that there was only me and this my hoard. And they would push me and laugh or scoop up handfuls of what is mine before they noticed the shadow."

Fenn swallowed the last morsel of chicken and put down her plate. She could imagine the men of her village, even Cedric, saying such things. Once, she would never have believed it of him, but she knew better now. She met Bryne's eyes. "Most of them never really see me either."

Bryne slowly unfurled her legs and rose to her feet. Fenn stiffened but didn't reach for the bone beside her. The dragon girl walked until she stood opposite Fenn. She bit her lip and hesitated before sinking to her knees. Her gaze was steady on Fenn's face, and, for some inexplicable reason, Fenn's cheeks started to heat. Flecks of gold like little sparks danced in Bryne's blue eyes. Fenn felt the dragon girl was looking directly into her, that her dreams, ambitions, and most private thoughts were laid open.

"If you want to leave, you can," Bryne said. She scooted so that her back was up against the wall; her shoulder lightly brushed against Fenn's own. "I won't stop you."

Fenn knew she should run. No one else had made it out of the mound alive, and if she returned unscathed, Ecberth would tell everyone of her bravery. She would be famous. Aeldorman Wulfgar would have no choice but to give her an armband.

But afterward, what then? After the gleam of her fame had worn off, what would become of her? Would Wulfgar give her a farm? No one in her village would accept such a wife. She would have to make it on her own. Sure, maybe the visiting bards would write a song about her, but she couldn't eat their songs or drink their praise.

Fenn had never considered what might come after she proved herself because she had never thought she would truly get the chance.

The dragon girl cupped her hands, and a tiny, fragile flame blossomed in them, illuminating the dark tomb. Her auburn hair glowed fierce red in the light. "Or you could stay here. For as long as you like."

Fenn gave Bryne the smallest nod.

Bryne rose and extended a hand to Fenn. "Let me help you up."

Fenn stared at the girl's fingers and at the yellow flames that licked the air between them. She hesitated and imagined the raw, blistered skin she had seen on Ecberth's shoulder. But if Bryne was trying to trick her, Fenn was probably dead anyway. She was trapped without a real weapon in a tomb with a dead king who had never been a useful warrior even alive. If she befriended this monster, the fallen men from her village might curse her. But they had ignored her all her life, and she had no real reason to think they were paying attention to what she did now.

She took Bryne's hand.

As cold as the ocean waves, the fire lapped against her fingers.

*   *   *

"Were you born this way?" Fenn asked. They sat together in the tomb's great upper chamber, on a bed of gold and gems. "As a dragon?"

Bryne shrugged. She picked up an emerald goblet, squinted at it, and then tossed it across the chamber. "You could say that. My family was cursed because our ancestor stole from the goddess Frythe while her back was turned. I thought it was just a story my mother told me to keep me in line as a child. My father was a Christian and he said her beliefs were nonsense. But then a I stole a necklace from a trader's cart, and, the next thing I knew, people around me were screaming."

"So, the curse was activated when you stole?" The story made sense to Fenn, as she had been raised in the old beliefs. Stories of monsters and curses had been as much a part of her childhood as Ma's beef stew. The gods had a wry sense of humor. Dragons were known to be thieves, creatures who lusted for gold. Frytthe had turned her back on Bryne's ancestor, and now no one could ever make that mistake again.

Bryne hugged her knees to her chest. "Once my body shifts, I can't control myself. The part of me that is dragon takes over, and I just react. I killed everyone in the market that day and I haven't gone home since, just in case my parents turn their backs before I can warn them. The aeldorman of my village vowed that if he ever saw me again, he would kill me."

Fenn scooted closer. The gold around Bryne seemed to pulse with gentle heat.

There were tears in Bryne's eyes, but when Fenn opened her mouth to ask how long ago this had happened, the dragon girl hastily blinked them away. She patted Fenn's hand and gave her a wry smile, then gestured to the sea of gems and coins around them. "As you can see, I'm a better thief now. I have a knack for finding gold."

Fenn chuckled, then stifled a yawn. She could not tell what time it was from deep within the mound, but her body was bone weary.

Bryne glanced toward the entrance of the tomb. "We should get some rest. It's late now, and they probably won't try to come back until morning at least."

Fenn reclined on the mountain of gold, then grimaced as the hilt of a dagger jabbed into her back. She tried, unsuccessfully, to fashion a pillow from an armful of coins.

Bryne rolled her eyes and pointed to the far corner of the chamber.

Fenn followed the line of her arm and noticed a pile of pelts. She gave Bryne a rueful smile. "That does look better."

Bryne bit her lip. "You'll have to sleep pressed up against the wall to be safe. And I'll sleep next to you, to prevent you turning over."

A blush crept up Fenn's neck and stained her cheeks. But she couldn't argue with Bryne's logic. If she was wedged between the stone wall and Byrne's body, she wouldn't be able to turn her back on the dragon girl. Besides, she had slept beside plenty of other girls. Before her elder sisters married, they had all shared a bed. She had never felt embarrassed or flustered by it.

Bryne led her across the room and watched as Fenn eased herself down onto the makeshift bed. The stone wall was cold and slick. Fenn shivered as she pressed against it as tightly as she could. Pinned like this, she wouldn't be able to run if Bryne suddenly shifted into her monstrous form. But when the other girl lay beside her and her impossibly warm body melted against the contours of Fenn's legs, she relaxed, and a smile tugged at her lips.

*   *   *

FENN WOKE, WARM TO THE point of sweating, with Bryne still curled next to her.

She sat up. Bryne stirred beside her and rubbed at her eyes. Fenn scooted toward the platter of berries that rested near their feet, careful to keep her back to the wall as she moved. Beside the platter, a golden armband lay half-submerged in coins. It comprised four braids of finely woven gold and was dotted with tiny diamonds. She fished it out and fastened it around her bicep.

"If I had so much gold, I could start my own hall somewhere," Fenn mused.

She would never have dared to give voice to that desire before, but here, her biggest dreams felt possible. She could make her own home, in a place where this one adventure didn't have to be the end of her story.

"We could start one together," Bryne whispered. She scrambled to her feet and walked to the other side of the chamber. The dragon girl seized the handle of a large chest. Its wood was rotted and blackened with age. She started to drag it back across the hills of treasure toward the place where Fenn sat.

Fenn got to her feet, but Bryne motioned at her to sit again.

"You have to be careful. You have to think before you move around me," she said, grunting with the effort of pulling the chest. "We'll always have to be careful."

By the time she reached Fenn, the dragon girl's skin glistened with a sheen of sweat. Exhaling deeply, Bryne kicked the chest onto its side. The lid fell open. Rolls of yellowing paper tumbled out, along with dark dried kelp and gray sand. The smell of the ocean, pungent with fish and salt, filled the chamber. Fenn breathed in the scents of her coastal home.

Fenn approached and unfurled the first scroll. It was a map, that much she knew, though she couldn't read the fine script etched across it. She'd had a few reading lessons, when the local Christian priest had offered, but her mother had worried he would try to convert Fenn, so she had stopped going.

She traced her fingers along the jagged coast depicted on the map. She didn't recognize any of the headlands or bays.

Bryne lay on her stomach beside Fenn and squinted at the map. She tapped a few places with a chewed nail. "I've been to many of these places already," she said. "Gathering gold for my hoard. Mostly from tombs and burial mounds—places where no one will miss it. There are places in these mountains where no one lives, whole valleys free for the taking."

"Aren't you afraid of the gods' wrath? Robbing tombs?" Fenn asked. A shiver passed through her. She was still concerned for her own soul's fate after desecrating Cyng Aella's bones. How much angrier would the gods be if she became a tomb robber?

"I've come to understand that the worst part of being cursed is being alone in it. Being what I am is not so bad in itself. I can fly!" She gave Fenn a shy smile. "And if the gods cursed us for this, we'd be together. We could build another hall in the shadow realm."

Fenn smiled back. It should have scared her, but people sang songs about the cursed too. The cursed were remembered. And what Bryne was offering her was a chance to continue her adventure, not settle down and be forgotten. If the hag goddess cursed them to wander the earth forever, neither of them would be alone.

Shouts echoed in the mouth of the tomb. Bryne turned to face it and her expression hardened. The fire coating her fingers turned brilliant blue.

"I'll go talk to them," said Fenn, brushing off her tunic. "Stay here and press your back against the wall so they'll all be in front of you."

"You should hide," Bryne hissed. Her gentle voice was ragged with panic. "You should go back down into the crypt with the skeleton and wait for me there. I will position the stone so there is no gap. My fire won't reach you, and, in my dragon's form, I won't be able to fit down the stairs."

Fenn shook her head. If Ecberth had come back for her, then she owed him a warning. She was not so naïve as to think that he would behave differently toward Bryne than any of the men before him had done. He and his warriors would dismiss her and, if she refused to come with them, they might grab her. Even if Bryne told them what she was, they wouldn't believe her.

They might not believe Fenn either, but she had to try. She had not seen Cedric among the bodies and still did not know for sure that he was dead. Even though he had dismissed her in the aeldorman's hall, they had shared friendship once, and that was worth something.

She backed away from Bryne, raising her hands. Eyes filled with tears, the dragon girl edged toward her. But it seemed Bryne did dare rise to her feet, lest she prompt Fenn to turn around and run.

"It will be okay," Fenn mouthed across the chamber.

"Fenn?" hissed a familiar voice from the darkness behind her. "Fenn, is that you?"

A strong hand reached out from the gloom and tugged her backward into the damp, cave-like entrance chamber. She tumbled into Ecberth's chest, and he enveloped her in a hug, before he stiffened and gently pushed her away.

The corpses that lined the walls had started to rot, and Fenn nearly gagged on the smell. She shivered as a breeze of cool air from outside whispered through the tomb.

"You survived, then?" Ecberth grunted.

Fenn grinned. "I told you I would."

"Didn't find the girl?" He sighed.

Fenn braced herself. "I did."

Ecberth looked down and scuffed his foot on the tomb's floor. He swallowed hard. "And is she…already dead? Are we too late?"

"She's inside."

A huddled group of shadows stood behind Ecberth. They held torches and iron weapons, and each wore thick black cloth covering most of their faces. One of the shadows stepped forward. He reached out and grasped Fenn's arm. She recognized Cedric's green eyes above the line of black fabric. He embraced her, and the familiar scent of woodsmoke filled her nose. She expected to feel relief and safety, but when he cupped her cheek and his gold armband brushed against her skin, her anger brimmed over.

"Thank the gods," he whispered. "One of our horses threw a shoe on the road and went lame. We arrived just after you did, and Ecberth told us what happened."

Fenn crossed her arms. "If you'd taken me with you, we'd have arrived at the same time."

Cedric laughed, a low rumble that echoed through her. Once, she had loved that laugh, had thought it sounded like thunder. Now it was a war drum to her fury.

She pushed away from him. "I am the only person who has entered this mound and survived. Now, if you all want to live, you should listen to me."

Cedric's eyes widened. Behind him, a few of his friends chuckled.

"You're small," Cedric said through ground teeth. "Perhaps you hid in some unlit corner while the beast prowled by. I would never hide. I would have confronted it."

"I did," Fenn growled. She turned back to Ecberth, ignoring the way Cedric's hand tightened on his sword hilt. "You have to listen to me. The maiden and the dragon are one and the same. She's cursed."

"Fenn," Ecberth said, his tone low and very gentle. "That may be what she told you, but do you think it's possible the girl has lost her wits? Who knows how long she has been in there alone with the monster, never seeing the sun? If the dragon has not returned, we should act quickly to rescue her now. A few weeks of food and rest, and she'll forget these delusions."

Fenn shook her head. It was this line of thinking that had gotten so many warriors killed already. "It's not a delusion. When I first entered the tomb, I saw her sleeping. I went to wake her and, in her shadow, I saw the dragon. I've talked to her—"

"Her? You've been talking to a dragon?" Cedric spat. He glanced over his shoulder at his friends. Their laughter, when it came, was nervous. "Maybe it's Fenn who has started to lose her wits."

Fenn's hands curled into fists. Cedric had been dismissive before, even defensive, after she'd bested him with swords or beaten him at Hnefatafl. But she had never heard him speak with so much venom.

"I have to admit," Ecberth said, each word slow and measured. "It does sound far-fetched, Fenn. Is it possible the dragon has put a spell on you? To make you believe such things?"

Of all of them, Ecberth's disbelief hurt the most.

"It's a curse," Fenn repeated. "She won't transform until you turn your back. Until then, she's just a normal girl. You can talk to her."

Ecberth sighed and rubbed his temples. His hands were coated with earth and sweat. Fenn wondered if he had even stopped to bathe since his first encounter with Bryne. She knew he was a good man, and he was trying. She had to make him understand.

Cedric's white teeth flashed in the torchlight; his grin was almost feral. "Well then, killing her will be easy."

He pushed past Fenn and ran into the tomb's main chamber with his sword drawn. He stopped and stared at the mountains of gold for only a moment before charging up the hill of coins.

Bryne sat where Fenn had left her. Her back was braced against the rear wall of the chamber, and her knees were raised to her chest. Her hands were submerged in the gold. Her red hair made a halo of flame around her pale face. Around herself, Bryne had arranged a circle of armbands, taken from the fallen. A torch sat beside her, and her winged shadow fell over Cedric as he raised his sword.

Fenn reacted on instinct. She raced after Cedric as he climbed, shouting at him to stop. Bryne was not a monster, and she had to make Cedric see it, if only for long enough so that she and Bryne could flee. She had glimpsed a possible future in the maps and she wasn't going to let him take it from her. Despite what the town, the aeldorman and Cedric himself had always believed, she had never seen such a future with him.

Cedric's eyes were clouded with confusion, and his scowl deepened as he searched Bryne's face for the truth of her curse.

He was too close to her now to see the outline of her enormous shadow.

"Stop and listen to me!" Fenn's heartbeat ratchetted, and she felt the drum of it in her ears. She flung herself between Cedric and Bryne and rounded on him. She bent down and grabbed a handful of the armbands. She threw them in his face. A rough gem sliced a cut beneath his eye.

Cedric went still. His eyes widened with terror, and he stumbled back, dropping his sword. His lips parted in a soundless scream and a trail of urine snaked down his leg.

A low snarl whispered in Fenn's ear.

*   *   *

FENN WHIRLED AROUND.

The dragon crouched behind her, as large as a drekkar ship. Its scaled hide was the deep purple of a midnight sky, its horns were white ivory smeared at the pointed tips with crusted red. Its massive jaws hung open, revealing double rows of sharp teeth, like the sharks Fenn had seen washed up on the beach. Slitted, reptilian eyes stared into hers. This creature was not Bryne. There was nothing human left in those eyes.

It unfurled its wings and screamed. Deep within its throat, orange fire bubbled.

Something gold, a plate or a crown, sailed over Fenn's head and connected with the dragon's forehead. The beast's attention snapped to the rear of the chamber. It squared its body and sucked in a deep breath.

Fenn grabbed Cedric's arm. Whatever he had said to her, she was not going to leave him to face a dragon alone. She hauled him under the dragon's massive wing as the beast rounded on Ecberth's warriors behind them.

As they slid into the burial chamber, the dragon turned its head toward Fenn. Something flickered in its expression: concern or confusion. And a tiny spark of hope ignited in Fenn that somewhere within the beast, Bryne had recognized her.

She didn't wait to find out.

At Fenn's command, Cedric lifted the heavy stone lid off Cyng Aella's coffin, exposing the steps beneath. He would not look at her. They jumped inside, and Cedric pulled the lid shut behind them. He was stronger than Fenn and was able to seal it from below, despite the angle.

Fenn prayed that Bryne, when she came back to herself, would not forget where they had gone. With the coffin's lid sealed, there was no light, and she knew there was no hidden way out of the tomb. They would not know that Bryne had transformed until she came for them, and Fenn doubted that Cedric would emerge again until he knew it was safe.

They collapsed against the stair together, shrouded in darkness. Cedric's breath came in short gasps. He reeked of urine and sweat.

Fenn touched his face and found that his cheeks were hot and soaked with tears.

*   *   *

"Do you think they're all dead?" Cedric whispered, what seemed like hours later.

His voice was hoarse with tears, and Fenn pictured the faces of all the boys who had volunteered with him. She had grown up with them, but they were Cedric's best friends, his brothers. But Ecberth had been *her* friend, in his own gruff way. He had given her a chance when nobody else would and had kept his promise to come back, after all. To imagine them all dead, incinerated as they ran, made her stomach clench.

And yet, imagining the alternative, that Ecberth and Cedric's band had prevailed and Bryne was dead, made tears sting her eyes. She bit her fist to muffle a cry.

They sat still on the stone steps, shoulders pressed together, listening. The tomb was silent.

"How long should we wait here?" Cedric asked. "I don't hear anything."

"I don't know," Fenn said.

Bryne had never told Fenn how long she remained in the dragon's body after she transformed. The beast could be coiled on its mound of treasure, waiting to ambush them as they emerged from the coffin. She wanted to wait for Bryne to come and get them, just to be sure, but if Bryne was dead or Ecberth's men had chased her away, they could be waiting forever.

Whatever had happened, Fenn needed to know the truth of it.

"I'm sorry," Cedric whispered, and she wished she could see his eyes as he spoke. "I shouldn't have said all those things to you. I just thought things were settled between us."

"I don't want to be your wife, Cedric," Fenn said, finally voicing the words she had thought a hundred times.

Perhaps if he, like Bryne, could have accepted Fenn for what she was and not what he wanted her to be, things might have been different. As it was, voicing her feelings after so many years concealing them made her feel light and giddy with relief.

She touched his arm and felt him tense.

He said nothing. A twinge of guilt twisted in Fenn's stomach, but she did not retract her words. Cedric would find someone else, and they would both be happier for it. Slowly, he shifted beside her onto his knees and, grunting with effort, pushed the coffin's stone lid aside.

The air was thick with smoke and ash. Fenn coughed into her sleeve as she emerged from the burial chamber. Cedric followed her, and together they crept into the tomb's main chamber. The smoke grew thicker, but when she squinted around, she could see no trace of the beast. A charred body rested beside the entrance; its mouth gaped in a grotesque final scream.

Crouching low and pressing herself against the wall, Fenn hurried forward into the tomb's entrance passage. Behind her, Cedric tripped over a chest and swore. His voice echoed. When they reached the warrior's burned body, he sank to his knees beside it.

Fenn expected to find the rest of Ecberth's band in the passage, but the only corpses there were days old. Heart racing, she sprinted up the hall. Ecberth had planned to wait outside the tomb, to trap the dragon as it emerged. Perhaps the lone warrior had sacrificed himself to get the beast's attention, in order to lure it outside into a trap. She imagined Bryne's body, broken and impaled, at the bottom of a pit. She ran faster.

The daylight struck Fenn's eyes. After days spent in the low light of the tomb, her vision danced with spots. She scanned the area in front of the tomb. Crows pecked at the skulls of the corpses, but none of them were fresh.

"Fenn?" a low voice hissed from the trees. A moment later, Ecberth emerged from the foliage. He wore no armor, but instead had sewn leaves and sticks to his tunic. His face was smeared with greenish mud. Behind him stood a group of warriors, all dressed the same.

Relief coursed through Fenn. Her knees trembled and threatened to buckle. She had not seen Bryne's body, and yet Ecberth was still here, alive.

"Why are you dressed like that? Where is your armor?" She asked.

Ecberth sighed. "We had hoped to lure the dragon out and catch it here. I had stationed half of our men on the other side of the tomb, and we had our arrows ready. But when we loosed, our arms didn't even pierce the beast's hide. We have only one choice. We'll have to track it and kill it when it transforms back into its human form. But it flew from here, and we have no tracks to follow."

Fenn thought of all the maps in the burial chamber, of the empty valley beyond the mountains they had found and planned to explore. She could picture the map so clearly in her mind. Bryne had told her that in the beast's form she had no control. She might not be able to think clearly enough to find it. But Fenn had seen that flicker of emotion pass through the dragon's eyes, and she believed that Bryne would go to the spot they had found and wait for her.

"You said you talked to it," Ecberth said. "Do you have any idea where it might go next?"

"No," Fenn lied.

Ecberth's eyes narrowed. "You're sure? You seemed quite... taken with it? Bewitched by it."

Fenn squinted out over the sacred field, toward the sea on the horizon. "She told me that when she was in the dragon's form, she had no control. The human part of her mind vanished."

This was part of the truth, and perhaps Ecberth heard that in her voice, because he nodded and clapped her on the shoulder.

"Bring a horse," he shouted to one of the warriors behind him. "Take her home."

*   *   *

FENN INSISTED ON RIDING IN the saddle, with her companion sitting on the horse's rump behind her. He was one of Cedric's friends, a gangly, red-haired youth named Aethelwan who, like her brother, had no skills in battle. She had been surprised when he volunteered in the Mead Hall, but his family still prayed to the old gods, and perhaps Aethelwan believed it was his only chance to impress Cempa.

She steered the horse down the path that led to the mountains and home. The mare trotted along placidly with her ears pricked forward. The horse knew that home would bring grain and comfort, a reprieve from the dragon smoke that hovered in the air around the tombs.

Aethelwan's grip around her waist was slack. Every so often, she could feel him jerk as he nodded into sleep. Fenn waited until she felt him sway, and then spun the mare in a tight circle. The boy fell in a heap at the horse's hooves.

He staggered to his feet. His face burned like a pyre, and he stammered, "Oh, um, I must have been sleeping…"

He tried to hop back onto the mare, but Fenn kept the horse moving in a circle around him.

"You know your way home, right?" she asked. She twisted in the saddle to point to the stream that bordered the path. "Just follow this for two days. It will you take you a village north of Lindeshelm, and you'll know your way from there."

"What?"

Fenn kicked the mare and sent her flying into a gallop.

"Fenn! Wait!" Aethelwan shouted, running up the path after them. "I'm sorry I didn't make Cedric take you before! Wait!"

She urged the mare on until the horse was slick with sweat and breathing hard. The track behind them was covered in hoofprints, and, even if Aethelwan tried to follow her, it would take him an hour on foot to realize she had not followed the path.

She steered the horse into the stream that bordered the track, then dismounted and patted the mare's sweaty neck. The cold water of the stream bubbled against her ankles. She slapped the mare's rump, and the horse trotted for home.

Fenn conjured a picture of Bryne's map in her imagination. She followed the stream until it widened and deepened into the Tilnoth, the river that cut the island in two. She stripped off her boots and fed them to the ripples. Then she climbed up the bank, onto the soft riverbed. The grass tickled her bare toes, but she moved as light as a deer, leaving no prints behind.

She shaded her eyes against the sun and stared up at the mountain ahead. On the other side of its peak, she would find Bryne and her next adventure. She smiled and began to climb.

ABOUT JULIA EMBER: Julia Ember currently lives in Seattle with her wife and their city menagerie of pets with literary names. She is the author of *The Seafarer's Kiss* and *The Navigator's Touch* (Duet Books). The duology was heavily influenced by Julia's postgraduate work in Medieval Literature at the University of St Andrews. *The Seafarer's Kiss* was named a "Best Queer Book of 2017" by Book Riot and was a finalist in the Speculative Fiction category of the Bisexual Book Awards. Her upcoming novel, *Ruinsong*, will be published by Macmillan Kids (FSG) in Fall 2020. Julia also writes scripts for games and is the author of several published novellas and short stories.

 duetbooks.com
 @duetbooks
 duetbooks
store.interludepress.com

an imprint of interlude **press**

Summer Love edited by Annie Harper

Summer Love is the first collection of short stories published by Duet, the young adult imprint from Interlude Press. These short stories are about the emergence of young love—of bonfires and beaches, of the magical in-between time when young lives step from one world to another, and about finding the courage to be who you really are, to follow your heart and live an authentic life.

ISBN (print) 978-1-941530-36-8 | (eBook) 978-1-941530-44-3

The Summer of Everything by Julian Winters

Comic book geek Wesley Hudson excels at two things: slacking off at his job and pining after his best friend, Nico. Advice from his friends, '90s alt-rock songs, and online dating articles aren't helping much with his secret crush, and when his dream job at the local used bookstore is threatened, he comes face-to-face with the one thing he's been avoiding—adulthood.

ISBN (print) 978-1-945053-91-7 | (eBook) 978-1-945053-92-4

The Camino Club by Kevin Craig

After getting in trouble with the law, six wayward teens are given an ultimatum: serve time in juvenile detention for their crimes, or walk the Camino de Santiago pilgrimage route across Spain over the summer holidays with a pair of court-appointed counselor guides. When it becomes clear the long walk isn't really all that much of an option, they set out on a journey that will either make or break who they are and who they are to become.

ISBN (print) 978-1-945053-97-9 | (eBook) 978-1-945053-72-6